I0775457

DRECK

DRECK

CLIFF JONES JR.

Copyright © 2023 Cliff Jones Jr.

All rights reserved. No part of this publication may be reproduced, distributed, or transmitted in any form or by any means, including photocopying, recording, or other electronic or mechanical methods, without the prior written permission of the publisher, except in the case of brief quotations embodied in critical reviews and certain other noncommercial uses permitted by copyright law. For permission requests, write to the publisher, addressed "Attention: Permissions Coordinator," at the address below.

ISBN: 979-8-8878502-1-4 (Paperback)

Library of Congress Control Number: 2023939953

Any references to historical events, real people, or real places are used fictitiously. Names, characters, and places are products of the author's imagination.

Book design by Allison Chernutan.
Cover illustration by Cliff Jones Jr.

Printed in the United States of America.

First printing edition 2023.

emily@fracturedmirrorpublishing.com
Fractured Mirror Publishing
Knoxville, Tennessee

www.fracturedmirrorpublishing.com

*Dedicated to my literary idol/eidolon
Philip K. Dick, who gave me the idea (and the
audacity) to write my own version of the Faust
legend, and to my wife Tina, who allows me
to approach the precipice of madness without
actually falling over the edge.*

PART 1
THE UNDOING OF FLIP FOSTER

In which a desperate loner plays with fire
And fans the flame of long-suppressed desire

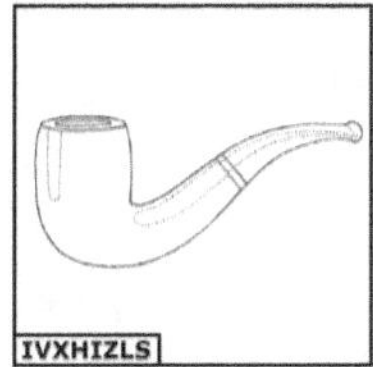

1. ENTER

IN THE CLOSET-SIZED OFFICE OF THE UNIVERSITY DORM, a wall-mounted phone sounded its third ring. Fourth. Fifth. No one in the attached common room could hear it over the din of acrobatic fighting, dramatic incantations, and cheesy music. The noise died down for an instant when the scene reached its climax, but then it came back in full force for the commercial break.

With an exasperated groan, Violet Valdez looked around the room. It was just her and her boyfriend Neil, who was on his phone busily establishing himself in the ecosystem of the latest social app. With much reluctance, Violet picked herself up from the couch and caught the office phone on its ninth ring: "Hello?"

The line was silent for a moment. Then just as Violet was about to hang up, the caller spoke in a tone somewhere between a sales pitch and a sexual proposition: "I'd like to speak to Dr. Frederick Foster, please."

"Doctor…No, I don't know anybody by that name. I think you have the wrong number."

Just then, Wayne Park entered the common room, eyeing Violet warily. He was the resident advisor this year, so the office currently belonged to him, and he was considering whether Violet had overstepped her bounds by answering his phone. She wasn't even a resident, after all.

Seeing Wayne, Violet gave a perfunctory wave and repeated back the name, more as a question to him than the caller: "*Frederick Foster?*…Nope, doesn't ring a bell. Sorry." Without another word, the caller hung up.

"Who was that?" asked Wayne.

"I don't know," Violet replied absently, her attention already returning to the TV. "Somebody asking for a 'Dr. Foster.'"

"You mean Flip? We *know* a Dr. Foster, remember?"

Violet was incredulous. "*Flip?* He's not a doctor; he's a student, right?"

"He has a doctorate," Neil broke in, finally looking up from his phone.

"That's right, in linguistics," added Wayne. "He's doing a master's in computer science now."

Violet was losing patience. The commercial break was just about over, and she really couldn't care less about Flip Foster's studies. "Anyway…the guy on the phone was asking for *Frederick* Foster, so…"

"Well, 'Flip' is probably a nickname," Neil offered. Violet shot him a cold glance, but his eyes were glued to his phone.

As if on cue, Flip Foster shuffled through the common room door, having gained entrance to the building in the wake of a noisy group of cap-wearing jocks. As usual, Flip had his laptop under one arm and an obscenely large energy drink in the other hand.

"Speak of the Devil!" called Wayne. Flip froze, obviously not relishing the attention. "Tell me, Dr. Foster, is 'Flip' your real name?"

He eyed each of them suspiciously in turn. "Real enough. It's from my middle name, Philip." He paused, deciding whether to volunteer any further information. "My first name's Frederick, but I never use it."

Wayne gestured to Violet, hoping to elicit some sort of apology for prematurely dismissing the phone call. But the show was back on. To indicate exactly how much she cared about Flip Foster's real name, she reclaimed her spot on the couch and turned the TV volume up a couple of notches.

Flip made his way to his customary corner of the room to plug in his laptop, and Wayne followed like a faithful dog. "There was a call for you just now, but Violet thought it was a wrong number."

"Hm," Flip grunted. In his experience, most calls were junk anyway.

Back on the couch, Violet was brooding, hardly paying attention to the show. "That guy is seriously tragic," she whispered to Neil. "Why does Wayne even let him in here? He doesn't *live* here. And he always smells like smoke."

"Well, to be fair," Neil pointed out, "you technically don't live here either." Then seeing Violet's face, he put down his phone and tried a different tack: "You know what he does here, right? He's a legit hacker. You can't do that kind of thing from your own place, you know. Too traceable." He added this last bit with a knowing smirk, as if he were an expert on the subject. "The guy's a genius! He helped me write this bot that's tearing through the SIA language courses. I can unlock whatever I want there, and that's really useful data. I'm probably gonna…like, make an app with it maybe."

Violet was unimpressed. "With a doctorate, you'd think he could get a good teaching position—if he were a *genius,* that is. Those who can't do, teach. You've heard that, right? And those who can't *teach*…well, I guess they just keep on studying until they can't get any more loans. And then…we'll just see how much of a genius he is *then.*"

Wayne watched as Flip set up his workspace. "So, what are you working on tonight?" He was too cautious to venture into the world of hacking on his own but assisted Flip however he could in exchange for the vicarious thrill of conquest.

"You know MeFirst?" Flip asked.

"Of course! I've been on MeFirst a few weeks now. It's pretty sweet. I get all kinds of free stuff, practically every day! I mean, you've got to opt into predictive purchasing to get the best bonuses, but hey, you can always resell the stuff you don't want."

Flip rolled his eyes. "You know how it works, right? You give them access to all your personal data so they can build a profile on you and guess what you might want to buy next. And at what price. Sure, you might get some discounts, but how do you think they make their money?"

"Well, I'm sure the…" Wayne began. And then with less confidence: "The stores they hook you up with? They pay to be listed?"

"Lots of companies pay MeFirst, but not for that. And not just private companies but political groups, government agencies… They pay for *your* information."

Wayne frowned. He felt more comfortable ignoring this obvious downside of Big Data. He'd have to tamp down his enthusiasm around Flip, ever the idealistic hacktivist. The guy knew his stuff, but he was kind of a buzzkill.

"I've got a MeFirst account," Flip continued, "but it's all fake information. I only access it here through a tunnel. I'm trying to escalate my permissions to see if I can pull data from other users. The only way to stop this kind of thing is to show people how invasive it is."

"Right…" Wayne said, somewhat dispirited. He didn't particularly *want* to stop MeFirst, but he wasn't going to admit that to Flip. "Well, I've got to head upstairs. I have a paper due in the morning."

"All right, you get some sleep," Flip said, pausing to take a pull from his energy drink. "I'll stay up and save the world."

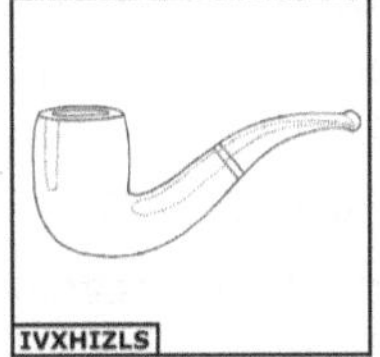

2. OPTION

IT WAS NEARLY MIDNIGHT WHEN FLIP BEGAN TO LOSE FAITH in his ability to crack the MeFirst data store. The web interface, at least, had turned out to be airtight. His next plan of attack was to go through old versions of the mobile apps to see if some outdated API exposed a vulnerability, but that wasn't likely to pan out if what he'd seen in the code so far was any indication.

No struggle, no progress, he kept telling himself—his secret mantra.

Three sharp knocks sounded at the dormitory's main entrance. Flip was alone in the common room, and the dorm as a whole seemed unusually quiet. He wasn't quite sure what to do. All the residents had keycards, so a knock at the door was rather unusual.

Cautiously—more out of curiosity than anything else—Flip stepped into the hallway and peered at the visitor through the glass door. It looked like…no, it had to *be* Levi Ferris! Founder and CEO of MeFirst Industries, a division of Triclave Consolidated. The man waved genially, as if they were old friends.

In a daze, Flip pushed open the door and said, "Can I help you, sir?" He regretted the "sir" as soon as it left his mouth. Ferris didn't look much older than Flip. But still, it did seem appropriate somehow. *Lucky Levi Ferris himself.*

"Dr. Frederick Foster," Ferris began. "At long last we meet." Lucky Ferris talked like someone out of a Dickens novel. This affectation meshed well with his trench coat, derby hat, and long scarf. The man was a billionaire. Eccentricity was expected. "Are you going to invite me in?" he continued after a moment. "I don't wish to trespass."

Returning to the common room with his guest, Flip suddenly remembered what he was doing when he'd been interrupted. In a panic, he leaped over and slammed his laptop shut.

Ferris smiled. "Don't play coy, Dr. Foster. We both know why I'm here."

Flip's heart raced, his hands began to tingle, and he was overcome by a sense of dread. "No, I honestly have no *idea* why you're here. How do you even know my name? I mean, I'm *nobody*." He had meant for this last statement to come off as casually self-deprecating, but it sounded more in the vicinity of pitiful and desperate.

"Come now, you called me here," replied Ferris. "You've been mucking about with my master account, trying to clone its permissions. Did you think I wouldn't see that?"

Flip sat down, visions of incarceration flooding his fevered mind. The justice system was not kind to hackers. He wanted to beg forgiveness and promise to never again poke around where he didn't belong, but he kept his cool just well enough not to admit guilt. Unsure of exactly what a lawyer might advise him to say, he said nothing at all.

Lucky Ferris continued: "Don't misunderstand me. I'm not here to condemn you. It's actually quite flattering. You think you'll find earth-shaking revelations in my database, do you? You entertain dreams of becoming the next Eddie Snowden? Hope you speak Cantonese." He grinned malevolently. "No, I'm here to offer you a deal."

Here he paused just long enough to make Flip sweat. Lucky held all the cards, and they both knew it.

"I'll give you what you want," he went on. "Full access. You just have to promise not to spill the beans to the media or the police or *anyone* for at least one week."

Flip couldn't believe what he was hearing. "But that's...*really?* And what do *you* get out of it?" he demanded.

Lucky Ferris feigned an exaggerated look of injury. "So cynical! I don't get anything out of it *directly*. I'm betting that after seven days you'll have learned enough to understand why blowing the whistle on MeFirst Industries would be a disaster. And then maybe you'd consider joining the team. We needn't be adversaries, you know."

Against his better judgment, Flip wanted to believe Ferris was sincere. And frankly, what alternative did he have but to go along willingly? Prison? Maybe, but worse still, he knew that if he passed up this opportunity, his curiosity would eat him alive. He'd been a student for two full decades, and each year he was left with more unanswered questions. The most salient conclusion he could draw from his studies up to that point was this: Nothing is understood half so well as people generally assume. No matter the field, more study is needed. Flip was tired of unanswered questions. He wanted to *know*.

In Flip's estimation, there was a great deal of esoteric knowledge purposely hidden from the general public, academia included. If he accepted the deal, he might be able to peer into that secret world of the ultra-elite. It would be within his power to access any information he wanted on practically anyone. Even those who hadn't opted into MeFirst tracking were undoubtedly being analyzed and cataloged by other means. This was part of what he'd set out to prove. What better way to test his theory than to peruse the data himself?

"Okay," Flip said at last. "Okay, seven days?"

Lucky Ferris looked positively giddy. "Right then," he said, producing a document from inside his coat. "I'll just need you to sign this. It's a standard non-disclosure agreement, boilerplate but legally binding. And because of the sensitive nature of our arrangement, I'll need it signed in blood."

Horrified, Flip wondered what sort of unholy pact he was entering into.

"Kidding!" Ferris laughed. "I'm kidding, of course. Lighten up, Foster! It's not like you're signing away your soul. Just keep this little matter to yourself for *one week*, and then…well, then it's up to you."

Once the agreement was signed (in ordinary black ink), Ferris showed Flip how to construct a rotating session token to bypass the normal security checks—salting the hash with the passphrase "n0n $3rv1@m"—and then…he was *in*. Simple as that.

While Flip was busy setting up his first query, Lucky Levi Ferris showed himself out, disappearing just as the clock struck midnight.

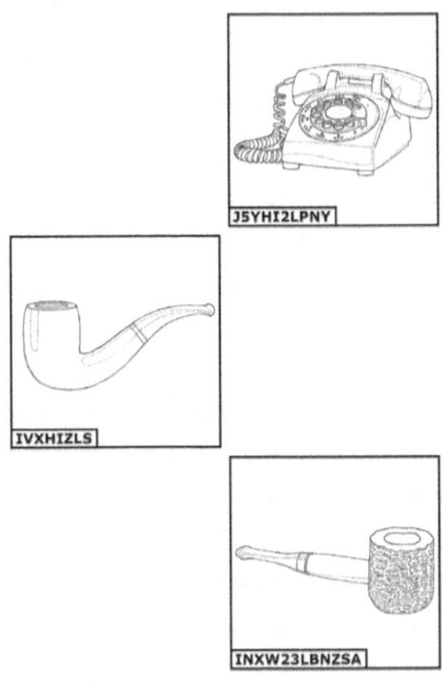

3. COMMAND

WHEN THE SUN CAME UP, FLIP HADN'T SLEPT A WINK. HOW could he? The more he explored, the more he longed to know. *How does the president act when the cameras are off? What's a party like at Dumptruck Dozier's mansion? How are things looking on the set of the latest Thomas K. Blick adaptation?*

After a few hours of bouncing around randomly between public figures, he began to explore the private lives of people he knew—digging and digging like some unruly chained-up dog. He learned that Violet basically hated him and thought he was a bad influence on Neil, Neil was an opportunistic narcissist who always took more than he gave, and Wayne…Wayne was a good guy, actually.

Next, his attention turned to people he'd known in the past. His mother, his father…his old not-quite-girlfriend Maggie Moon. He hadn't seen her since high school graduation, nearly ten years ago. Once he started catching up on Maggie's life since then, he found it impossible to stop. Unlike back then, he could now see the full picture: emails, browsing habits, photos, conversations, *everything*.

He learned that Maggie's mother, a breast cancer survivor, was now fighting pancreatic cancer—and losing this time. He saw how she'd helped her hyperactive little brother get over a serious addiction to painkillers only to lose him overseas in the never-ending War on Terror. She'd had only one serious relationship since high school: three years, but no kids and no ring. She held a B.A. in English literature, which was of only slightly more interest to employers than his own Ph.D. in linguistics—that is to say, none whatsoever. Her best friend was currently a long-haired cat named Martha.

With all this extra context, Flip's obsession with Maggie developed into something he considered at least a reasonable approximation of love. Drunk on his newfound abilities—and mildly insane from lack of sleep—he committed himself to finding a way to get Maggie back. In her position, she ought to be glad to reconnect with a semi-successful old flame—regardless of how they'd parted.

Neil poked his head in the door and gaped in disbelief. "Flip? You've been here all night?"

The sudden interruption came as a shock and pulled Flip rather unpleasantly down from his reverie. "No! I mean…well, yeah, I've been here." He didn't look back at Neil as he spoke. He was too busy minimizing incriminating windows.

When it became clear that Flip wasn't planning to add anything further, Neil said, "So…I guess I'll see you later then." Flip's presence wasn't really so unusual. He was sort of the dorm's mascot, the antisocial hacker always parked in the common room. Many of the residents were undoubtedly under the impression that he worked there, performing some uninteresting technical task for the university.

"Yeah…" Flip replied, turning at last with a wild-eyed grin. "I guess time kind of got away from me! I'm about to head home. Later, man."

Neil didn't seem particularly convinced, but he raised his eyebrows and put out his hands as if to say no explanation was needed. "Later," he said and continued on his way.

On his own again, Flip began to seriously consider what to do next. Since he'd made the deal with Levi Ferris—nearly eight hours ago—he'd just been wandering through the wilderness of cyberspace in a fog, without any clear purpose. His full attention had been on testing out his new godlike abilities. The eventual focus on Maggie had been merely an extension of that, seeing how much information he could gather on a given individual.

But even recognizing this underlying motivation, he couldn't shake the feeling that he belonged with Maggie Moon, that he *deserved* her. And now he finally had the power to do something about it.

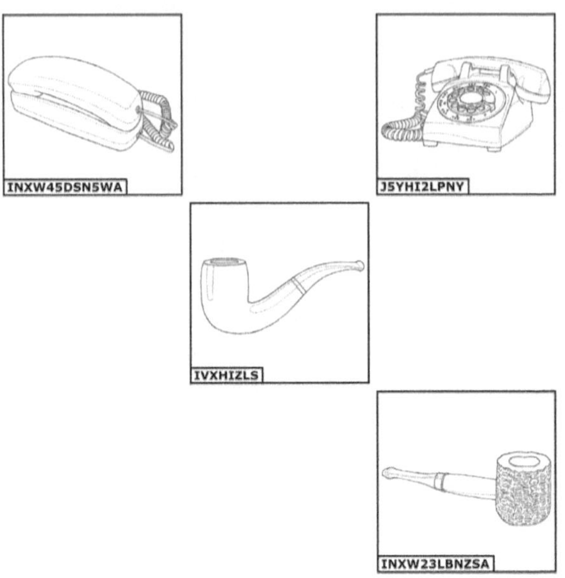

4. CONTROL

IT WAS HALF PAST THREE IN THE AFTERNOON WHEN FLIP woke up back in his apartment. He'd missed both Thursday classes already—not that he'd really planned on attending. His Fridays were more or less open this semester, so he could easily devote the next several days to MeFirst. And to Maggie.

The repetitive action of building queries for the MeFirst API had quickly become automatic habit. It had followed Flip into his dreams, as habits tend to do. In that otherworld, he'd run queries on himself—an obvious idea in retrospect, but one that hadn't occurred to him while he was awake. He couldn't recall any specific information he'd turned up on Frederick Philip Foster of Philadelphia, but the whole dream was so unpleasant that he felt a strong aversion to trying such a thing in his waking life.

No, today would focus on one Margaret Elaine Moon. Flip knew from his research that Maggie was working at Elysian

Fields, a vegan restaurant near Germantown. She was currently reading Goethe's *Faust,* so he picked up a copy as a conversation starter. She seemed to be an avid reader with tastes ranging from George Eliot to James Tiptree Jr.

Considering it a worthwhile investment, Flip spent the afternoon getting an overview of several books he could pretend to have read. He fully intended to read them all eventually, so he didn't feel *too* bad about the deception. Actually, he realized, he'd have to get pretty comfortable with deception from here on out. There was no going back to how things were before he'd met Lucky Ferris.

He *had* met Ferris, hadn't he? For a moment, he considered the possibility that the whole encounter had been all in his head, nothing more than a waking dream. But how else could he have gained master access to MeFirst's full, unencrypted data store? The knowledge had to come from somewhere.

When Flip arrived at the restaurant forty-five minutes before closing, he made a point not to look anyone too closely in the face. He put thoughts of Maggie out of his mind for the moment. It was important that she see him first—and all the better if she saw him reading his copy of *Faust.* The book gave him a perfect excuse not to notice her serving a nearby table. In the blur of his periphery, he saw Maggie glance over several times before hesitantly approaching to say hello.

"Flip Foster?" she asked, as if she weren't already sure. "Wow, it's been a long time. How are you doing?" She looked back and forth between him and the book, trying to gauge the right moment to point out the coincidence. Flip hesitated for an awkward instant, giving Maggie just enough time to blurt out, "I'm reading that same book!"

"What? *Faust?*" Flip said with a blank expression. Then he faked a sudden recognition: "Maggie! You look exactly the same! Sorry, you just caught me off guard. So you decided to stay in Philly after all? Can't believe I didn't run into you sooner! It's a big city, I guess."

"Well, I did move away for a while," she said, "but after college…" She looked back to the kitchen. "Hey, I've got to get back to work, but we should catch up soon."

Flip pretended to interpret Maggie's politeness as a direct invitation: "Well…sure, why not?" he said with mounting enthusiasm. "What time are you off?" As if he didn't already know.

Maggie raised an eyebrow. She was nobody's fool, but Flip wasn't playing fair. "Give me like half an hour," she said with a reluctant grin.

It was surprisingly easy to pick up where he'd left off with Maggie—minus the teenage drama. They were adults now, independent and fairly well educated, though Maggie had apparently given up the academic life for her present career in food service. They both had more important things to worry about than who installed a keylogger on whose computer and whether he had or hadn't used her email password. That was all in the past.

Once they had settled in at a nearby coffee shop, the conversation turned from obligatory pleasantries and updates to the book they were both reading: "I loved Part One, but honestly, I'm having trouble with Part Two," Maggie said, pausing to sip. "Like, are they supposed to be time traveling or something?"

Flip saw his opportunity, and holding back a predatory grin, seized it: "I read that Goethe took a break between the two parts and visited Italy. It seems like that really affected the story. Part Two was more in the style of a classical epic poem." He hadn't actually read a word of *Faust,* but he'd gone through several commentaries, which in many respects made him more of an expert.

Maggie nodded. "Okay, that makes sense. It kind of reads like a dream."

"He must have really been affected by all that history," Flip continued. "Rome. Can you imagine?" He knew she could—*had,* in fact, many times. Maggie stared back at him in contemplative silence. It was working. "I've been planning to do some traveling myself," he went on. "I think I'm going to take some time off from my studies and teach English in Switzerland, for a year or two. I've always wanted to live there."

Maggie sat up straight, her eyes widening. "That sounds *amazing*. The Alps! I've actually thought about teaching there myself. What an insane coincidence!" She smiled warmly and sipped her caffe breve.

Flip's conscience manifested itself as a rising sense of dread, which he gulped down with a mouthful of red eye. *This is fine*, he told himself. *I'm fine. I shouldn't feel guilty for knowing things. Since when is knowledge a bad thing?*

Since the Tree, Flip heard in the background noise of his mind. *Since Eden.* He ignored this intrusive thought and focused back on the matter at hand.

Maggie's smile softened into an inviting little grin, and Flip held her gaze for just a bit longer than etiquette would dictate. Now they were getting somewhere.

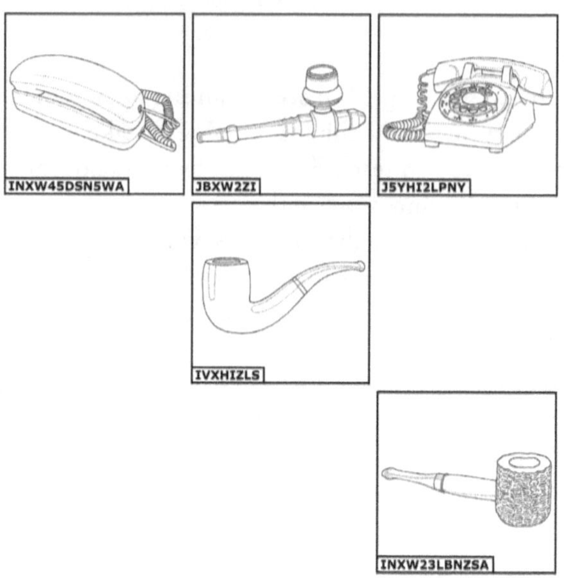

5. HOME

AROUND ELEVEN THE NEXT MORNING, FLIP PULLED BACK
into the parking lot of Elysian Fields. It was a bold move, yes,
but he and Maggie had really hit it off the night before. Besides,
Flip only had a week with full access to the MeFirst data, so he'd
have to move fast rekindling the old flame. In a few days, he'd be
working without a net.

Maggie showed up for the lunch rush at five minutes to
noon. Flip was just finishing his "Tempeh of Poseidon" bowl,
which had turned out to be a much heavier meal than he'd
expected. He struggled to suck any remaining bits of kelp out
from between his teeth before Maggie spotted him, but it was a
small restaurant, and he was not entirely successful.

"Back so soon?" Maggie asked with a smirk.

Flip gulped down some water, wishing he could use the straw
to pick his teeth. But alas, it was too late. "Maggie Moon! Fancy

meeting you here," he replied weakly. This he followed up with a nervous titter and some incoherent mumblings to the effect that she probably thought he was stalking her.

"No, I don't think that," Maggie laughed. "I *know* it! It's pretty obvious, really. Unless you just decided to turn vegan last night and have no idea how to cook for yourself."

"Okay, okay…" said Flip. "You got me. Actually, I realized after you left last night that I forgot to ask your number."

Of course he already had Maggie's phone number, but he needed to actually *ask* her for it before he could use it. All of the information he got from his MeFirst access had to be filed away in a special compartment of his brain, separate from the ordinary things that he could safely admit to knowing. He was getting so much practice in this sort of context-dependent amnesia that it was starting to become automatic and effortless. At that moment, he probably could have passed a polygraph saying he didn't know Maggie's phone number, hadn't memorized it while running through a wide range of cold-call scenarios.

Maggie wrote down her number and suggested they meet up again later for a walk in the Chestnut Hill area. "We've got a lot more catching up to do," she said.

The next day was Saturday, and Maggie was off work, so they had their first real date—at least that's how Flip thought of it. They spent a while exploring the beautifully chaotic Magic Gardens and then headed down to Harbor Park around sunset. All the ever-shifting multicolored lights hanging from the trees made the place feel otherworldly, like a psychedelic dream. But as the evening wore on, the crowds got to be a drag, so they went back to Maggie's place for drinks.

Before Maggie could get her keys out, a woman in long braids answered the door. "Oh. You must be…Flip?" she said with a grin. "I'm Laila. I was just leaving." She threw a bag over her shoulder and slipped out in a hurry.

So that was Maggie's roommate. There was something about her that drew Flip's attention despite being in the middle of a date that was going really well. It was like he already knew Laila somehow, from somewhere he couldn't quite place. *Another life maybe.*

They hadn't been in the apartment five minutes when Maggie got a call from her mother. She took it to her bedroom and left Flip alone with the liquor. *Should I wait?* he wondered. *How much is acceptable to drink on my own like this?* After some deliberation, he settled on two fingers of bourbon and a splash of Frangelico.

As he quietly perused Maggie's bookshelves, Flip kept an ear trained on the bedroom door, more out of reflex than any genuine interest in the conversation. With his level of MeFirst access, he could listen to the whole thing later if he wanted to. And when Maggie eventually called it a night, politely showing him the door, Flip headed over to Wayne's dorm so he could do just that.

"Hi, Mom. How are you feeling today?" Maggie's voice sounded in Flip's earbuds with that distinctive audio quality reserved for phones and drive-thru speakers.

"Hi, sweetie! Well, you know, I'm taking it day by day. How are you?" Flip increased the playback speed.

"Are you sure you don't want me to come out there tomorrow? It's no trouble."

"No, no…your dad's taking good care of me. He's taking a few weeks off from work, actually."

"Oh, that's great! Is that paid leave?"

"Well, it's…no, he's already used up the *paid* time. But we're doing fine; don't you worry about us. I'm actually calling to see how *you're* doing. Any news with your stories?"

"No, nothing yet."

"You working on any new ones?"

"I'm sort of…doing research for a new one."

"Oh, very *intriguing!* What's it about?"

Maggie laughed a little nervously. "I'm not exactly set on that yet. Something about social media. How it's, you know…

worming its way into everything these days. It's like…you can't just turn it *off,* you know? Like Lookbook…"

"Oh, your dad *loves* Lookbook. I can't heat up a can of soup without a photo turning up online! He makes such a fuss."

"You know I tried two different times to quit Lookbook? I closed my account—as much as they *let* you close it—but then there's always some reason I have to go back. This time, at work, they told me…you know if you're a business, you *have* to have a Lookbook presence, so they told me to manage the page because I'm the most tech savvy. Like it takes a rocket surgeon to manage a Lookbook page."

Rocket surgeon? Flip cracked a smile.

"So to manage the page…" ventured Maggie's mother, "you have to have an account?"

"Right. And then when I went to set up a *new* account, with a different email address and everything, they made me verify my identity through my phone. And then on my new feed, there's all the content from my old account, all the stuff I told them to get rid of! They never delete a *thing.* It just keeps growing and growing, consuming our lives and turning them into more of itself, an endless stream of inane updates, political rants, selfies, memes…and all that dreck's just gonna stick around, what… *forever?*"

"Well…nothing lasts forever, sweetie."

"Hey, Flip." It was Violet. Hearing his own name just then had startled Flip into slamming his laptop shut and yanking the buds out of his ears. Obviously pleased with this reaction, Violet grinned and added, "Watching porn in the common room, eh?"

"No! No, I wasn't watching…that," Flip sputtered. "I was just concentrating…on my work."

Violet laughed at his feeble explanation. "You ought to concentrate on being less of a creepy weirdo, man." She did have a point.

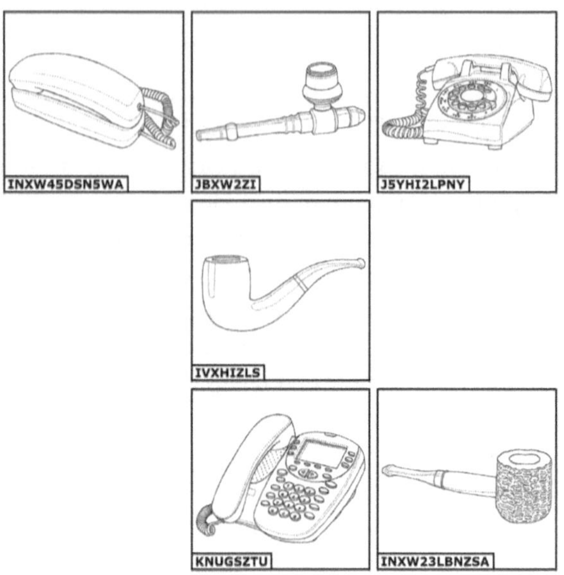

6. SHIFT

BY SUNDAY AFTERNOON, FLIP HAD RESOLVED TO GIVE UP his access to the MeFirst data store a few days early. All that free-flowing information had been instrumental in winning Maggie back, but he didn't want to push his luck. If Maggie ever found out what he'd done, there would be no hope of repairing the damage. Besides, he didn't want to wait for Wednesday night to see what would happen when the seven days were up.

The trouble was, Flip had no way of contacting Levi Ferris directly. Just emailing MeFirst felt like a bad idea. But for all Ferris knew, Flip was still planning to leak some cache of incriminating data to the media. Honestly, there was no chance of that now, not after he'd built a relationship on the private information he'd technically stolen from MeFirst. What a lousy excuse for a whistleblower he'd turned out to be.

Then an unsettling possibility occurred to Flip: *What if Ferris had expected this?* Flip knew firsthand how easily people could be predicted and manipulated if only you had the right data. And Lucky Ferris had it *all.* Surely something so obvious as Flip's desire to reconnect with Maggie Moon would not have been overlooked. Flip seethed with impotent rage as he realized he'd been playing right into Ferris's hands all along.

Could a smooth operator like Lucky Ferris really be trusted to honor his end of the deal? For that matter, what had Ferris actually promised? He'd hinted at some kind of job offer but never really said anything concrete. And how could Flip *accept* a job at MeFirst anyway, knowing what they were doing to the world? Through various forms of deception and blackmail, they held virtually unchecked power. Practically every celebrity, politician, and academic with any clout was under their thumb.

There would come a time—and Flip hoped it would be soon—when diligent citizens banded together to reject MeFirst and its ilk. But how? The information was out there for the taking, voluntarily supplied for the most part. The U.S. could pass a law forbidding companies from buying and selling personal information, but what did the laws of one nation amount to in the world at large?

If politics was the art of getting other people to do what you wanted, then MeFirst was a formidable political body—one that had existed in one guise or another long before the U.S. was founded and would likely go on well into the future. It was a leviathan that had outgrown its masters and could no longer be killed.

So Flip's course of action was clear. He couldn't work for MeFirst, and he didn't have the heart to fight them if it meant losing Maggie. He'd have to run. Would Maggie join him? That was a lot to ask, and she'd need some sort of explanation. What could he tell her? More lies, probably. If only he could be sure that Ferris would leave him alone. But no, people with that much power didn't hold onto it by showing mercy.

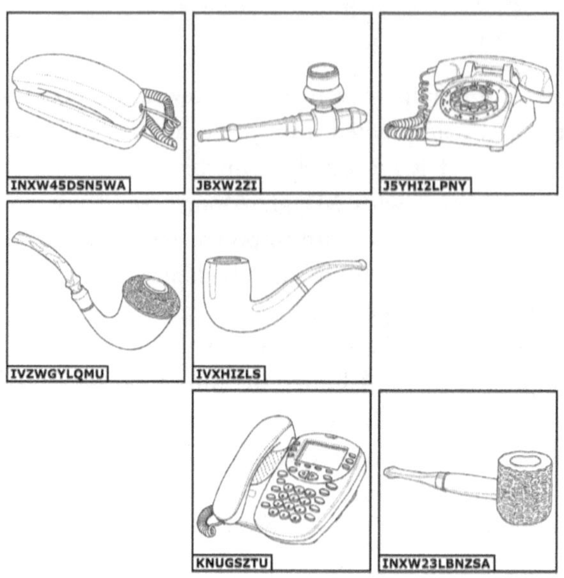

7. escape

AS FLIP WATCHED, HIS LAPTOP COMPLETED THE FINAL pass of its secure wipe. Back to its factory settings, it was now a brand-new machine.

"Wayne?" he called out.

Wayne Park got up from his desk with the weary groan of a man twice his age. Visibly worn out from a long study session, he ambled over to Flip. "What's up, man?"

"I'm going to be leaving for a while," Flip answered. "Maybe a long while. I want you to take this laptop and do something good with it."

Wayne looked puzzled. "You mean like…hacking? I don't know; that's not really my…"

"*Something* good," Flip interrupted. "It's up to you to decide what's good. You probably know better than I do."

With that, Flip said goodbye to his only real friend and set out for Elysian Fields. He'd seen this coming for days, even if he was only just now admitting it to himself. He was leaving town, probably for good. Everything he'd be taking with him was already on his back. Frederick Foster would soon disappear forever. But on the plus side, so would his massive student debt.

Heading uptown on his moped, he stopped off at the Schuylkill River and surreptitiously tossed his phone into the water like a fleeing murderer disposing of an incriminating weapon. As he watched it disappear into the river's murky depths, he considered the possibility of taking that path himself. He knew he didn't deserve Maggie's affection or anyone else's, not after what he'd done. And this was a secret he'd have to keep year after year. He could never come clean, not in this world. But maybe in the next?

Flip stood there a moment taking in the view, the wind off the water, and the cool blue moonlight suffusing it all with an eerie, otherworldly calm. Turning his back to the breeze, he carefully packed a bowl and struggled to light up his pipe as tears rolled down his cheeks. He'd been so stupid. Such a selfish, arrogant prick. Wouldn't the world be a better place without him in it?

No, he decided. Killing himself wouldn't do any real good for anybody, least of all himself. If there were such a thing as a fair and just afterlife, it would not be a pleasant place for Flip Foster. And if there were *no* afterlife at all…well, that possibility was even more horrifying. So Flip would just have to go on, trying to do more good than harm, day by day. He couldn't undo his wrongs, but he could recognize them and try to guard against adding on more.

When he arrived at Maggie's restaurant just before closing, he didn't feel like going inside. He just waited in the parking lot next to her car, silently going over the things he needed to tell her—and the bits he still had to hold back.

Maggie was the last to leave Elysian Fields. She waved awkwardly to Flip, keys jangling, and proceeded to lock up. As she walked closer, she made out Flip's pained expression, and her face fell in response.

The two stood facing each other in silence for a moment until Flip finally muttered, "I need to talk with you. It's pretty serious."

"Follow me home then," Maggie said flatly. Determined not to let her anxiety get the better of her, she'd slipped into that calm, almost apathetic persona Flip knew so well from their high-school relationship.

Back at Maggie's apartment, Flip sank down into the living room sofa and stared at the words on its lone throw pillow: "As soon as you trust yourself, you will know how to live."

Despite all his preparation, he found nothing to say. Martha, the shaggy gray cat he knew from countless ill-gotten photos, walked up and rubbed against his ankles. When he reached down to pet Martha's head, she leaped into his lap, nuzzling his chest and purring with delight. Flip's eyes welled up with tears, and he didn't bother to wipe them as they fell. Maggie sat down beside him and took his hand in hers.

"I really messed up bad," he said at last. "I wish I could tell you *everything*, but…I really can't."

Maggie raised an eyebrow and pursed her lips. Then she sighed and said, "Well, whatever it is, it'll pass. I'm here with you now. I'll help you through it." Flip didn't doubt she would *try* if he put her to the test, but she had no idea what he was up against.

"I need to leave the city," Flip said gravely. "I have to change my name and be off the grid for a while. Will you come with me?" He stared into Maggie's eyes, without guile this time, simply wishing to understand and be understood.

Maggie's brow furrowed as she tried in vain to imagine what could possibly warrant such a reaction. "Well…*no*, of course not. I can't abandon my whole life and go live out in the boonies with you. I have responsibilities. My mom has stage four cancer. Do you know what that means? I—I can't just abandon her."

Flip had expected an answer along these lines. It wasn't fair of him to ask. "I'm sorry…" he said. "I didn't mean it. I mean… can I just stay with you for a couple days?"

"Well…" Maggie hesitated. "The sofa folds out."

It was clear that the carefree honeymoon period was over. Their interactions were now tinged with a faint melancholy, like the echo of some shared tragedy. They soon fell into a comfortable routine, as if they'd been living together for years. Flip never explained what sort of trouble he was in, and Maggie never asked. Laila mostly kept to herself, rightly sensing the delicacy of the situation.

When Maggie got home from work on Wednesday night, they didn't watch a show or talk or anything. Maggie just climbed onto the sofa bed with Flip, and they held each other in silence. After around half an hour, her breathing became faintly audible, and Flip knew she was asleep. It was ten minutes to midnight.

Silently, with immeasurable care, Flip extricated himself from Maggie's arms, got out of bed, and gathered up his things. Martha jumped into his path as he made his way through the kitchen, so Flip held out a hand for her. She rubbed against his fingers from her nose to the tip of her tail and then wandered off again like their business was complete.

Flip crept as quietly as possible out the front door, leaving Maggie asleep on the bed. Climbing onto his moped, he hesitated one final moment, searching for some other solution to the mess he'd made. Finding none, he rode off into the night.

In the chill darkness of the pre-dawn hours, Flip rode steadily westward on the Pennsylvania Turnpike. Almost on a whim, he took a right turn into the woods and headed north awhile. He hoped somehow to lose himself in Amish country, though he had no concrete plans to that effect. He wasn't even sure how to go about finding a genuine Amish community, not just a tourist town selling Amish goods.

He stopped for gas on the edge of a town called Quentin. Inside the convenience store, the clerk seemed to be closing up for the night. The "open" light in the window blinked off as Flip approached, and the door was locked when he tried it. You had to pay in advance this late at night, and the pump only accepted credit. He'd counted on paying in cash, reserving his credit card for only the direst of emergencies. As Flip stood debating whether to break his "off the grid" rule or camp out until the store reopened in a few hours, a black van pulled up beside him.

It struck him as odd that the van would pull into that particular spot when there were other pumps available, but before he'd even had a chance to get nervous about it, the door slid open, and two men wearing Guy Fawkes masks jumped out. The taller of the men ran toward the store while the other aimed a pistol at Flip's head. And then…the world seemed to fold in on itself. Everything fell away and scattered like ashes in a strong wind.

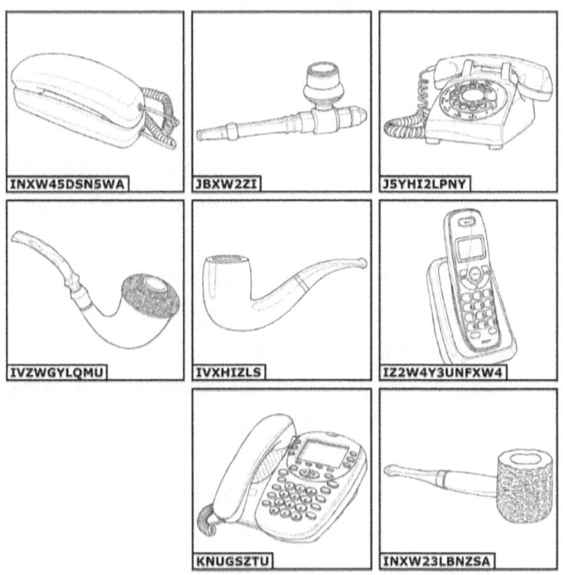

8. FUNCTION

"MIS-TER FOS-TER...MIS-TER FAAAWSS-TURRR..."

Flip opened his eyes to see a familiar purple Magic Eye poster tacked onto the ceiling above his bed. He crossed his eyes slightly. It was a yin-yang. The 3D was inverted since he hadn't used the recommended viewing method, but...how much did that really matter with a yin-yang? He was in his old dorm room. *Old?* Now, why had he thought that? He'd only ever had the one dorm room. *But yeah, I guess it is kind of old.*

He checked his wristwatch. 10:10 p.m.

"Flip!" His roommate Lucky slammed both of his hands down onto the edge of Flip's mattress. "You up, man? I know you ain't trying to go to bed already. Not *tonight!*"

Flip rubbed his eyes and forehead, stifling a yawn. "What's so special about tonight?"

Lucky beamed, delighted that Flip had taken the bait. "*Beltane,* man! It's, uh…Irish, I think. But even better than Paddy's Day. It's like Mardi Gras meets Halloween!"

"Okay, I'm up. I just, uh…I don't actually remember falling asleep. I was having some weird dreams. I can't quite remember…"

Lucky was already pocketing his keys and wallet, heading for the door. "You can tell me all your hopes and dreams on the way. Come on. It's later than you think."

"Where are we going?" asked Flip, pulling on a pair of socks.

"Where else, man? The Pyramid Club!"

"The what?"

"You'll see." Lucky winked and threw on a black derby hat.

Flip just smiled, shaking his head. *What a poser.*

After a few minutes of walking, it became clear that they weren't heading to Lucky's car. "How far is this place?" Flip asked.

Lucky stopped walking and cocked his head to one side. "Come on. You've got to know the Pyramid Club. It kind of stands out."

Flip shrugged. Maybe he did remember a "Pyramid Club." It certainly sounded familiar. But when they'd walked a mile or so and they were crossing the Schuylkill River, Flip began to see their destination rising up in the distance. It was an *actual* pyramid, right in the middle of Philadelphia! Smooth and black, embellished with glowing purple lines and baroque clusters of neon symbols, the structure totally dwarfed everything else in the area. This was *not* something Flip had seen before. "What the hell, man. That's…What *is* that?"

"What's it look like?" Lucky answered with a smirk.

"But…what happened to the ESP?"

"The what?"

"You know, the old prison in Fairmount? Didn't it use to be right there?"

Now Lucky gave a shrug. Either he was hiding something or…no, Flip was all mixed up. The prison he was remembering looked like some kind of medieval fortress. No way that was real. Okay, it was coming back now. How could he have forgotten the Pyramid Club?

"Sorry, man," he told Lucky. "I've still got some cobwebs in my head from that nap."

"You know the cure for that?" Lucky raised a thumb to his mouth, grasping an invisible bottle and making a drinking motion. "Fix you right up."

They both laughed and pressed on through the chill night air. When they finally made it to the Pyramid Club, it was already after eleven. Flip wondered what day of the week it was but decided against asking Lucky since that would probably get him mocked for worrying about being out on a school night. Better just to go with the flow and enjoy himself.

Despite the club's unique exterior, it was actually pretty standard fare inside. Colored spotlights, disco balls, an energetic DJ playing bass-heavy remixes of radio tunes. Some of the patrons sported animal-themed accessories, even a few masks, but this was hardly the wild bacchanalia he'd been promised.

Sensing Flip's disappointment, Lucky clapped him on the back and said, "Come on. We're hitting the bar, and then we're going up to level two."

"Don't they have a bar on level two?"

"Hell yeah, they do," Lucky said with a laugh. "But you've got to drink here first. Them's the rules!"

So they stopped by the bar, where Lucky ordered them each three shots of Old Scratch whiskey. Flip threw back the first ounce. It wasn't half bad. But as he gulped down the second and third shots in quick succession, he thought, *It ain't half good either!* He might have made this joke aloud, but the music was so deafening that no one would have heard anyway.

Lucky closed out the tab and presented the six empty glasses to the bartender. In exchange, he and Flip both received three hand stamps in the shape of an owl. This gained them admittance to level two of the Pyramid Club, but only for the night. The bouncers, Lucky informed him, were inflexible and utterly humorless about protocol.

"So it's three shots and then right up the stairs?" Flip asked, only half joking. "No elevator?"

"No struggle, no progress," Lucky shot back with a wink.

As they passed through the velvet rope leading to the stairway, Flip thought he glimpsed a familiar face in the swaying throng behind them. "Was that…Maggie Moon?"

Flip had only made this remark to himself, and Lucky shouldn't have been able to hear it, but he nonetheless responded: "You've got to let go of the past, man. Maggie's not coming back."

Before Flip could ask what that was supposed to mean, he was knocked to his knees by a laughing woman in long braids. She'd just passed the rope and was deliriously happy to be making her way upstairs. And drunk as well. She was clearly drunk.

"Oh my gosh. I'm so sorry, dude!" She grabbed Flip by the arm and pulled him up like he weighed nothing at all. The woman smelled of cigarettes and sweat, but with pleasing secondary notes that drew him in unexpectedly. Long after she'd continued on her way, running up the stairs in zig-zag fashion, Flip continued to breathe slowly and deeply, subconsciously hoping for another whiff of chemical euphoria.

He never caught it though. The air was heavy with a smoky olive oil scent, a bit stifling though not altogether unpleasant. This was due to the countless burning torches that lined the stone walls of the stairwell. They were its only source of light. The overall effect reminded Flip of the medieval fortress that he'd imagined—*dreamed?*—had once stood on this spot.

The second level of the Pyramid Club was somehow even louder than the first. There was a live band onstage, a punk group Flip hadn't heard of called "Black Dog." Two mohawked singers were growling out incomprehensible lyrics to the tune of "Für Elise." This level was like a totally different establishment. Most of the crowd here looked rough and ragged compared to the primped-up party people on the ground floor. They pushed their clothing to such bizarro do-it-yourself extremes that they seemed to be making fun of the very idea of dressing up. But ironically or not, they were dressed with every bit as much fastidious care as the people below them.

Flip thought he could stay and dig this scene awhile, but he was already getting curious about level three.

"I know what you're thinking," Lucky yelled over the noise. "What's on level three?"

"How'd you do that, man?" Flip yelled back.

"Deal with the Devil!" This response, obviously meant as a joke, struck a sour note with Flip. As it echoed in his memory, he couldn't escape the feeling that it sounded like a command.

They crossed the dance floor (really more of a sway-and-jostle floor) and found the entrance to the next stone stairway. Before they could proceed, they had to take off their shoes and deposit them behind a counter. They were each given a numbered ticket, along with a warning: "If you lose your ticket, you're going home barefoot."

Level three was noticeably smaller than the others, a result of climbing higher up the pyramid. Despite the reduced space, it was far less crowded than the lower levels had been. The air was hazy with smoke, both tobacco and otherwise. A quintet played mellow jazz in one corner. The floor was a black-and-white checkerboard, and long purple curtains lined the walls. Most of the floor space was taken up by small wooden tables topped with stained-glass lamps—each unique in design, but all in shades of red, violet, and blue. It reminded Flip of the dream sequences on that show *Twin Peaks*, but with a slightly expanded palette.

"This is more like it!" Lucky said, spreading out his arms as if to embrace the whole scene. Then he added, "Now if you'll excuse me, I've got to go powder my nose," and headed off to the restroom.

Flip walked over to the bar, taking an open seat next to an older man in a blue suit. As soon as he did, the man turned and introduced himself: "How do, son? The name's Tommy." He stuck out a hand, which Flip felt obligated to shake.

"I'm Flip."

"Flip?" Tommy repeated back. "Like…'The Devil made me do it!'" Still grasping Flip's hand, the old man laughed and wheezed like he'd just made a hilarious joke.

Flip forced a smile, certain he was missing something. "I'm… sorry, *what?*"

Finally breaking the handshake, Tommy asked, "Flip Wilson? No?"

"Oh, right…him," said Flip. "Yeah, I've heard of him. He was just kind of before my time."

"Aw, hell. A classic ain't before *anyone's* time," Tommy replied with a noticeable slur. And then thinking this over, he added, "Yeah…yeah, I guess he was though."

Flip ordered a Sazerac, and the two of them just sat there quietly listening to the band play John Coltrane's "I Wish I Knew."

"You know…" Tommy said after a moment. "The people that run this place…They want your mind, your soul, and your body. You really shouldn't be here. You ought to stick to places they can't find you. You know? Be strategic."

Flip had no idea how to respond to this. He sipped his drink to buy some time, and then thankfully, Lucky returned from the restroom before the awkwardness became unbearable. Without another word, Tommy left his money on the bar and shuffled off toward the exit.

Just then, Flip spotted the woman who'd knocked him down in the stairwell. She was kneeling in front of a roped-off passage to level four, receiving some kind of mark on her forehead. Flip gulped down the rest of his Sazerac, snatched a twenty out from under Tommy's empty glass, and placed it under his own.

Lucky observed this boldness with obvious delight. "I could have paid for that, you know. Ah, but you're independent, a self-made man."

Flip only grunted, trying to get to the woman before she disappeared into the stairwell. But again, he was too slow. She was gone before he'd made it ten feet. He turned back to Lucky. "I want to check out the next level, okay?"

"You want to check *something* out," Lucky teased. "All you've got to do is ask. But I don't recommend getting mixed up with Laila Duchamp. She's headed nowhere fast."

"You know her?" Flip asked, surprise dulling his embarrassment.

"Sure, man. I get around."

Flip didn't have the time or the patience to unpack that remark, so he just walked over to the velvet ropes and got in line.

"I'll catch up to you," Lucky called to him from the bar. "You have fun."

The line was short, so it didn't take long to reach the double doors. Two colossal guards stood with a woman in a red cloak between them. She was the only one actually interacting with the guests.

"Kneel, please," the woman told Flip. He complied, and she continued: "Do you wish to proceed to level four?"

"Yeah," said Flip. And then, "Yes."

"Do you agree to abide by any and all club rules?"

Flip wasn't exactly sure what those rules might be, but again he said, "Yes."

"Do you acknowledge the reality that you are not the flower, only the dirt?"

Hm… Why not? "Yes."

Immediately, she uncapped a fat permanent marker and drew a black X in the middle of Flip's forehead.

That's going to be tough to explain tomorrow. But honestly, he didn't much care about tomorrow at this point. He wanted to see Laila again—to smell her, talk to her, maybe even touch her. And even more than that, he realized, he wanted to know what was at the very top of the pyramid. He'd already come this far. It would be a shame not to see it through.

Level four of the Pyramid Club was every bit the wild party Flip had been looking for. And quite a lot more, actually. He saw things that simultaneously fascinated, enticed, and repulsed him. In the center of the floor was a small bonfire, which heated the surrounding area to an alarming degree. Despite this, dozens of people danced happily around the blaze, many of them blowing into flutes or panpipes. Clothing was apparently optional—and not particularly encouraged by the excessive heat.

Flip searched the merry revelers for Laila, who was nowhere to be seen. Gradually, he concluded that she must have passed through this level already, quickly ascending to the next. And so, partly to catch up with Laila, partly out of curiosity and pride, and partly because level four made him uncomfortable to an extent he wouldn't have believed mere minutes ago, Flip resolved to move on once again. He walked over to a nondescript door with a single bouncer standing next to it. The man looked uncannily like Laurence Fishburne in *The Matrix*, right down to the mirrorshades.

Without moving a muscle to acknowledge Flip's approach, the man asked, "You wish to proceed?"

"Uh…Yeah, sure. What do I have to do this time?"

"Very simple," replied the man, producing a small purple pill.

"I'm supposed to take this?" Flip asked. "What is it?" And then when it was clear he'd get no answer from the man, he added, "What, I don't get to choose between red and blue?"

Without even cracking a smile, the man replied, "Your choice is to take it or leave it. What does the color matter?"

"No, I was just—" Flip stammered. "That was…a joke." No response. "Haven't seen that one yet, eh?" Nothing.

Obviously, Flip had arrived at a crossroads. He could turn back now, get some sleep, and try to figure out how to get the permanent marker off his forehead in the morning before class— or he could swallow this mystery pill and head up to level five of the Pyramid Club. Judging by the size of level four, there might only be five levels total. The floors had been getting progressively smaller, but that might easily have been some architectural trick. There were no windows anywhere, so the building could conceal any number of hidden rooms and passageways. The pyramid had certainly looked taller than five stories from the outside. But why all the secrecy? What was all this structure and protocol *for* anyway?

Flip stared down at the thin white line separating level four from the stairway to level five. If he'd been just a little more clear-headed, he might have gone on considering such questions awhile and possibly even concluded that taking an unidentified drug from a creepy stranger dressed as Morpheus was probably a bad idea. But he was drunk and in a hurry, so he took the pill, crossed the line, and climbed the stairs.

Unlike on the previous floors, the torchlit medieval style of the stairway didn't abruptly change at the top. The room looked more like a dungeon than a dance club. It was poorly lit, musty, cold, silent, and completely empty. Except...no, there was someone sitting in the shadows of a far corner. Flip was suddenly terrified. Why had he left Lucky behind on level three? For that matter, why had he gone out at all tonight? He'd been sleeping so soundly, dreaming of...

"Flip? Is that you?" It was a girl's voice—or a woman's, maybe his own age. It sounded familiar, like someone he used to know in high school. No, it couldn't be.

"Maggie?"

She stepped forward into the torchlight, dragging behind her a heavy chain clasped around one ankle. "Thank God," she said tearfully. "What's going on? Are you going to get me out of here?"

Flip stumbled backward, unable to process what he was seeing. "What—what *is* this place? I—I—I'm not supposed to be here."

"You? What about *me*?!" Now she was getting angry. "What about Martha, huh? They killed my cat, Flip! How could you just leave like that? Who are these people anyway?!"

This is crazy, Flip told himself. *This is all in my head.* He backed up a few steps, edging toward the stairwell.

"Where are you going?" Maggie asked, her voice suddenly small and fearful. "Where are you *going*?!"

Flip clambered down the stairs, trying to outrun Maggie's echoing screams. He wanted to call for help, but first he had to get out of this place. Once he was safe, he'd go to the police.

But would he though? He was on some kind of drug. Was it affecting him yet? Was he just imagining Maggie up there? Why her? They hadn't seen each other in years, but she was talking like…She had a cat named Martha. It was gray. How did he know that?

After running down what felt like far more than enough stairs to get back to level four, Flip's vision began to blur and his head felt suddenly heavy. He slowed his pace, but his body demanded rest. Involuntarily, he sat down on the cold stone and drifted almost immediately into a numbing cocoon of sleep.

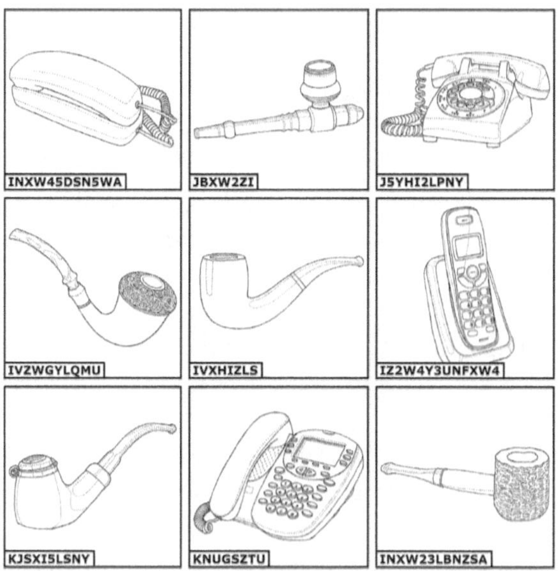

9. RETURN

FLIP WAS SEATED IN A LEATHER ARMCHAIR, UNMOVING AND uncaring. His head throbbed painfully, and his mouth tasted faintly like molasses. With a start, he remembered the encounter at the gas station and reflexively checked his hands and feet for bindings. To his surprise, he was unfettered, at least in that respect.

A few feet in front of Flip's chair was a small wooden table with another armchair on the far side of it. He sat up and reached for the table, but his fingers collided with a transparent partition he hadn't noticed. It was only visible now from the smudge his hand had left on the glass. Just then, a door to the right of the table opened and a familiar figure strode in.

"Dr. Foster!" said Lucky Ferris with a smile. "A pleasure to meet with you again; it really is." He casually seated himself at the table as if he were about to conduct a brief interview.

"Lucky…" Flip croaked with some effort. He tried to say more, but his throat felt raw, and nothing in particular came to mind.

"Yes," continued Ferris. "You're lucky to be alive. Now let's get down to business. What were you doing so far from home last night? I expected you'd be in your usual spot, where we met a week ago."

"I…" Flip struggled to gather his thoughts, but all he found were vague self-recriminations: *I crossed so many lines. I'm a monster…*

"I said seven days, Dr. Foster. Was that not clear? I meant *precisely.*" Ferris let his annoyance show on this last word, but only for an instant.

Flip's response was less than coherent: "I didn't know you'd… I'm not—I mean, I'm not going to tell anybody…I didn't find anything good, you know?"

"It seems to me you found exactly what you were looking for," Ferris replied. "You've no doubt destroyed all record of your immoral and illicit activities on your end. But surely you don't imagine MeFirst wasn't watching the whole time, keeping a nicely detailed account of each and every incursion. We've got it all. It's our *business.* You, on the other hand, have nothing to show for your efforts. Only what I allow you. I give, and I take away. Do you understand?"

Flip nodded gravely. Wiping his computer and tossing his phone into the river didn't seem like such a good idea in retrospect.

"You work for me now," Ferris continued. "Technically, you've been a MeFirst employee since you signed the contract a week ago. You've made a fair attempt at erasing yourself from the world. If you'd prefer, I can provide you with the means to finish the job and be done with it." He paused here with a hateful grin. "But if you ever get any more of those ridiculous notions of becoming some kind of Robin Hood vigilante, redistributing information as you see fit, just remember you're a *part of it.* In up to your eyeballs. MeFirst operates within the law; *you're* the criminal here."

In a strict, legalistic sense, Ferris was right. Flip could almost believe he'd been wrong about everything from the start. MeFirst was a corporation, a legal fiction. Its only moral obligation was to make money for its shareholders. In accordance with the law, customers were notified that the price they paid was not money but their own privacy. *Buyer beware.*

But no. That was bullshit, and he knew it. Legal fictions were just that: fiction. At the end of the day, it was always human beings who were responsible. The tools they employed, the code they wrote, the rules and regulations and chain of command… None of these layers actually absolved anyone. They only muddied the waters so the guiltiest parties could pretend they'd done nothing wrong.

Flip spoke up, now with conviction: "I can't work for you, sir. Not if I want to live with myself. If you want to throw me in jail, then I guess that's how it'll have to be. If you want to kill me, then…you should know I left a detailed confession with a reporter I know—to be released in the event of my death." That sounded like a good idea, actually. Flip wished he'd thought of it sooner.

At this, Ferris's eyes flashed with a moment of fiery rage followed by a mocking laugh. "Well, it was worth a shot," he muttered. "But if I can't persuade you to join the company, then we've reached something of an impasse. Surely you're aware I can't let you go free, not with everything you know. Even if I wanted to, it's just not within my power."

Flip opened his mouth to object, but no words came.

"I'm sorry," Ferris said with unexpected compassion. "You're between a rock and a hard place, and that's where you're going to stay."

Then he stood up and exited his side of the room. Simultaneously, a door to Flip's right opened, held by a well-dressed woman who looked as if she'd be more at home in a bank than a clandestine interrogation chamber. Beyond the door, an ordinary workplace hummed and buzzed with activity. Dumbfounded, Flip followed Ferris through a maze of cubicles until they reached the elevators.

Along the way, he'd considered trying to get an employee's attention so he could call for help, but he felt insubstantial somehow, not at all in control. He was just swept along in Lucky Ferris's wake like some inanimate object, observing but not interacting. He walked automatically, without feeling.

The elevator doors opened, and they stepped inside. It was surprisingly dim. When the doors closed and the elevator started moving, Flip couldn't tell if it were rising or falling. The overhead light flickered and winked out. Now thoroughly disoriented, he questioned whether he was even inside an elevator at all. It was cold and dark and suddenly breezy. As his eyes adjusted, he began to make out a familiar structure up ahead.

"Why is it s-s-so cold?" Flip asked.

"Cold? Nonsense. It's the middle of spring! *Beltane,* man." With that, Ferris turned and jogged up a small stairway to a set of glass doors, delivering three sharp knocks. After a moment, he smiled and waved through the glass.

One of the doors opened, and an oddly familiar voice asked, "Can I help you, sir?"

"Dr. Frederick Foster," Ferris replied. "At long last we meet."

PART 2
SECOND SIGHT

In which a woman gives up everything
And finds at last her lost engagement ring

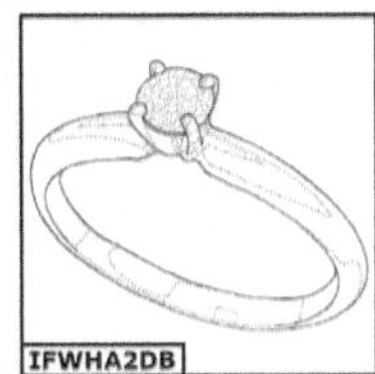

1. alpha

IT LOOKED LIKE AN ORDINARY CONTACT LENS. AT A CERTAIN angle, it took on an odd greenish cast, but there was really nothing about this small, curved disc of hydrophilic polymer to hint at its true potential, its ability to remake the world by altering the perception of millions. Second Sight was poised to be the hottest item of the upcoming holiday season, nothing short of a revolution in sensory input augmentation—or as it had come to be called in recent months, "SIA."

Laila Duchamp held the smartlens between her thumb and forefinger, lifting it into the light and flexing it gingerly. Neil Conrad looked on from his desk, supervising. He had instructed her to stress-test the product thoroughly before beginning her official trial.

The two of them held the same position at Triclave International and were hired within a month of each other, but Laila was fairly certain Neil considered himself her boss. Laila didn't want to come off as lazy or argumentative, so she usually just did as he asked. What else could she do?

"You're sure squishing the lens like this won't damage it?" Laila asked.

"Well, if it does," replied Neil, "that's something we'll want to note, right?"

Laila turned to check the man's face for irony. As usual, it was completely blank, unreadable. If she hadn't known better, she'd have sworn Neil was a stolid, meditative introvert, keeping the bulk of his thoughts and feelings to himself. But no, Neil voiced his thoughts freely enough. There just weren't all that many of them.

Laila continued, "What I mean is…if this thing gets damaged, and I stick it in my eye…isn't that kind of risky?"

Neil took a moment to show all due consideration before answering: "I hear your concern, and you know…I *get* it. But we're QA. That's what we've got to do. If Second Sight's going to have some kind of negative effect, we have to find that out now. We can't leave it to a bunch of kids on Christmas morning."

He had a point. Unwelcome, but still valid. The quality assurance team had to do its best to break products like Second Sight, to send them back to the drawing board if need be. Laila exhaled a sigh of resignation and positioned the device in her left eye. At first, everything looked more or less the same. Then she blinked five times in quick succession to start it up.

All at once, Laila's vision had an uneven, flickery quality, almost like she was wearing a pair of those old red-blue 3D glasses. But instead of one side having a red tint and the other blue, each of her eyes now perceived a subtly different world. Everything in her left eye had so much more depth to it, more clarity and contrast. Independent of lighting conditions, the darkest color in view was a deep black, and the lightest was a brilliant white.

Laila tested this effect by closing her right eye and cupping both hands over her left. The wrinkles of her hands were clearly visible, if a bit lacking in color. Perfect night vision. This feature on its own would guarantee a demand for Second Sight.

In order to avoid the jittery feeling that came from wearing only one lens, Laila kept her right eye shut. She now observed the subtler effects of the product's infrared thermal imaging. Neil and his laptop possessed a neon vibrance that rose and fell rhythmically. The pace of this pulsation corresponded to temperature, so Neil's was much faster than his laptop's, and cooler items like the desk and chairs were comparatively drab, reduced in saturation and lacking any discernible pulse.

Neil leaned forward expectantly and asked, "So what's it like?"

Laila frowned as she positioned the other lens in her right eye. "You don't have yours in yet?"

"Well…no, not yet," Neil said with a blush. Through the smartlens filters, his cheeks throbbed with a vermilion glow. "I thought I'd let you try it first. Seemed kind of risky."

2. Smoke

ALL AFTERNOON, LAILA KEPT HER LENSES IN FOR THE official alpha trial. The experience was intense, but not entirely unpleasant. It was actually kind of fun, like her life had just been turned into a video game. She was still a little nervous about what side effects she might suffer from this "augmented visual experience," but so far she hadn't found much to complain about. Second Sight was delivering exactly as promised. Everything looked fresh and crisp and new, beating and pulsing with life.

Laila's visual field was now saturated with layers of information she'd never even known she was missing. She was already beginning to take certain filters for granted: high-contrast, autofocus, motion tracking, night-vision, zoom, blink-repair, mood mapping, thermal, wide-angle, edge-enhance…It felt like she'd been living her whole life in a dark cave and was only today given the chance to step out into daylight.

Ironically, it was sundown before Laila was actually able to step outside. Second Sight wasn't the only thing on her plate, and the new lenses didn't help at all with her on-screen work. If anything, they slowed her down because she kept getting distracted by more interesting sights around the office. There were a few things she could have done without seeing, in fact. Like the time she left infrared on in the bathroom.

On the drive home, Laila gave in to a sudden whim and pulled off the tollway onto an unfamiliar side street. This part of town was not nearly so well lit as the elevated freeways and megamalls she was used to, but with her smartlenses normalizing brightness and contrast, it may as well have been broad daylight. She found herself approaching Yancy Park, a little patch of forest in the midst of the city—the perfect place to really put Second Sight through its paces.

The park was officially closed for the night, so Laila pulled into a homeplex across the street, in a space reserved for "future residents." Up and down the street, the only signs of life were behind closed doors—faint pulsing lights inside their homes, all unaware of Laila's presence.

It was truly amazing, this view that Second Sight provided. This was more than entertainment; it endowed her with new confidence, a sense of mastery over her surroundings. She'd never even realized how powerless she felt without the lenses. But now, she owned the night.

Only the parking lot of Yancy Park was fenced off. The rest of the property was just surrounded by trees, which were easy enough to pass through. As a teenager, Laila had visited this park after hours countless times with her friends, though never before on her own.

After making her way through the foliage and onto the main brick path, she came to a thin stream of flowing green specks stretching out a hundred feet or so before disappearing into the woods. *Leafcutter ants!* There had to be thousands of them carrying those tiny leaf scraps back to their underground nest.

Once Laila figured out how to use her phone to work the zoom on her lenses, she was able to inspect the tiny creatures as if they were just inches away from her face. The effect was strange and disorienting—actually a little nauseating—so she didn't keep it up for long.

Laila passed under the barren limbs of live oaks and cedar elms, staring up at a perfectly full moon. The face in it looked kind of like Elvis Presley—on a bad night. She shifted her focus to this single light source, and everything else darkened. And then looking away, the scene returned to its former clarity. It was all thoroughly mesmerizing.

She closed her eyes and watched the darkness brighten to a neutral gray. The musty ozone smell of the city vied for dominance with varied fragrances of earth and vegetation. It was up to the wind to decide the victor. And then suddenly, she smelled cigarette smoke. It was stale and acrid and oppressively heavy, as if emanating from unwashed clothing.

"Hey, *wump*," growled a hoarse voice from behind her. Startled at this intrusion into her reverie, Laila spun around to see a roughly dressed woman with a black stocking over her face. Something about the way the woman held herself told Laila she meant business. And then she noticed a knife in the woman's hand, which would probably have been convincing enough on its own. Grinning through the fog of her makeshift mask, the woman continued, "What you got for me?"

Laila couldn't think straight. This was her first mugging—or whatever this was—and she didn't know how to react. *What is it I'm supposed to do?* she asked herself. *Kick her in the crotch? No, that's probably just for men. Scream? I doubt that would do much good out here. I'm not even supposed to be out here. So I guess I'm a criminal too. But not violent. That's a good point. This woman would obviously win any kind of fight I might put up. Just give her what she wants!* "I—I don't have any cash," Laila stammered at last. "You can check my—"

"Ain't nobody got cash no more. And I *don't* take CredShare.

Look, I'm just begging for scraps here. Just give me whatever jewelry you got and we're square." The mugger gestured with her knife, pointing it toward Laila's emerald engagement ring.

"I swear that's all I have, and it's really not worth much. Maybe a hundred credits. It's just the sentimental value for me because—"

The mugger laughed. "A hundred creds? Maybe that ain't much to a one-percenter like you, but it sounds pretty green to me. Give it here."

Oh God, not the ring. I'm not ready for that. What else do I have on me…? "My phone! That's worth more than the ring. Take it!" She held the device out hopefully.

The masked woman wasn't having it. "You think I'm brainless? You know they're tracking you on that thing, right? Everything you do. That's how come they're so cheap." She edged the blade closer to Laila's face. "Nah, you give me what I *asked* for, or you're gonna get cut. And then I'll probably just take it anyway. Come on, wise up, wump."

Laila took off the ring and handed it over. What else could she do?

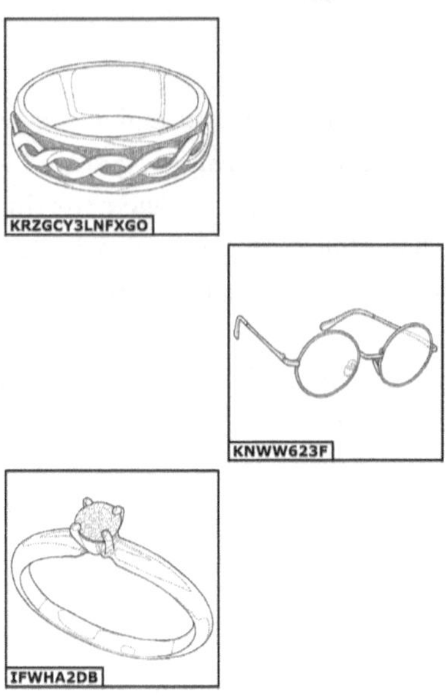

3. TRACKING

THE NEXT MORNING AT WORK, LAILA GOT A SURPRISE visit from Levi Ferris, head of product for Triclave International. With a warm smile, Levi asked, "How are you feeling today, Laila? All good?" And then before Laila could come up with something resembling an answer, he added, "Come on, let's talk in my office."

Once the door was shut and they were both seated, Levi said, "Well, I have good news for you. With our help, the police have already apprehended the woman who attacked you last night. You'll have to identify her yourself, but that's really just a formality since we have her on camera. Caught her in the act!" Levi looked so pleased with himself you'd have thought he'd been the one to personally chase down the fugitive and slap her in irons.

"What do you mean you caught her in the act? Nobody—"

Then all at once, Laila flashed onto the true power of Second Sight. "So there were…there were cameras in the park?"

"Well, a few, but they weren't much help," answered Levi. "I'm talking about the *product*. We got a nice faceprint with the new tech."

There it was. *Laila* was the camera. "But…I never saw her face. She had a mask."

"Well, it wasn't much of a mask," Levi laughed. "The spectral signature came through just fine."

"Wait, I'm confused…" Laila didn't want to believe what she knew perfectly well already. "My lenses…You can see what I see? Like *all the time*?"

Levi lifted an eyebrow and sighed wearily. "I'm guessing you didn't read the terms of service?"

"I'm sorry, I must have missed the—"

"No, don't worry about it. You're fine," said Levi—as if Laila were the one in need of forgiveness. "Second Sight isn't marketed as a camera because that introduces privacy concerns. But of course, it *has* to be a camera. That's how it works. The feed is processed in real time and projected back onto the retina. To reduce lag, we offload that processing onto the user's paired device. And from there…Sure, it's accessible—but *only* to parties with a legitimate interest."

"Which includes…?"

"Law enforcement, yes. Whenever a crime is committed… This is a perfect use case, actually. And you're the very first to demonstrate Second Sight's effectiveness in the wild! This is really going to help our Series B funding."

Laila didn't know what to say. In a few short months, Second Sight would go live in thousands of homes across the country. And then if all went well, adoption would spread to millions worldwide. The whole planet would become one big interconnected web of cameras. It was all too much to fathom, this writhing, seething mass of digitized human lives—this mocking, sneering leviathan. Laila couldn't breathe.

What am I doing here? she screamed inside her head. *I'm part of the problem working for these unfeeling robots. They're trying to reduce us all to safe little reflex machines, extensions of their own will. But who's at the top? Who's not a machine? Are there any authentic humans left?!* Then she remembered something that made her feel a little better, at least. "So the police have my ring?"

Levi's smile vanished. "Unfortunately, no. Your assailant has been…less than cooperative. If only we had more eyes on the ground, we could have tracked her better and seen what she did with that ring, but as it is…We've won the battle, but we're still fighting the war. We're building a new world here, you know? Full visibility. No more shadows for the cockroaches to hide in." And then with a conspiratorial grin, he leaned in and whispered, "We're turning on the lights."

Laila nodded and smiled back. What else could she do?

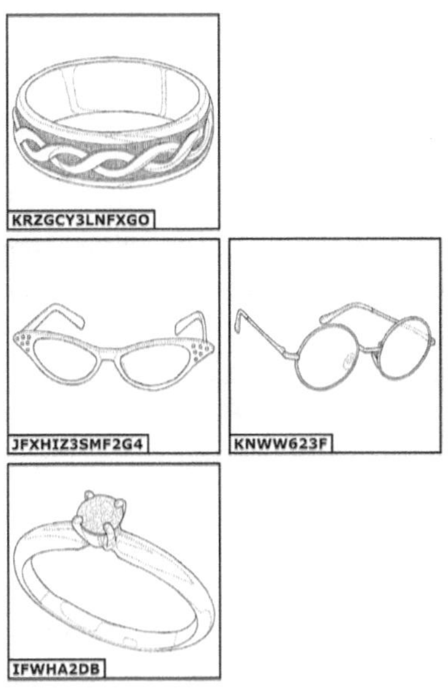

4. INTEGRATION

CHRISTMAS CAME, AND WITH IT, A NEW ERA OF SIA adoption. It was no longer just a handful of transhumanist bodymod freaks but a mainstream cultural shift. Laila made use of Second Sight just like everybody else, but she couldn't shake the feeling that she was being watched. And not just in the sense that she was monitored and cataloged like everybody else. No, she felt scrutinized beyond any reasonable expectation. She often found herself closing her eyes for extended stretches of time, especially in the bathroom.

Dr. Violet Valdez, Laila's company-provided therapist, told her that all this was normal, an expected aftereffect of her mugging and the loss of her personal property. It was very common to feel violated, dehumanized, exposed. Still, it felt bigger than that to Laila. But as Dr. Valdez pointed out, "We can hardly be expected to see ourselves objectively, especially in matters of the mind."

It was on Dr. Valdez's advice that Laila decided to take the loss of her engagement ring as a sign from a higher power and finally ease back into the dating world. It had been nearly two years since the crash. Twenty-two months of solitary mourning. That would have to be enough. Laila knew she'd never love anyone else the way she loved Flip, but that was okay. She would just have to find someone who'd understand that, someone who wouldn't be jealous of a ghost. Every night in her dreams, she was back with Flip, and she didn't intend on giving that up. But in the morning, he always slipped away again, leaving her waking life that much lonelier.

This was where Wayne came in. There really wasn't anything about him that stood out to Laila as especially attractive or endearing. He just seemed like a nice, friendly guy—not disgusting, not brainless, not ideologically infuriating. They both frequented Grindhouse Coffee in the old downtown, and when she used Second Sight to match his face with a Lookbook profile, nothing too crazy came up. Most importantly, he was *there*, and he said yes when she asked him out. So just like that, Laila found herself eating Persian food with Wayne Park, a man she'd only just realized was essentially a stranger.

"The thing about Flip was he got excited about everything," Laila told him. "You could catch him off guard with some topic he didn't really care much about, but then he'd get to thinking about it, and before long he'd *start* to care. Pretty soon, he'd be telling you all about it, you know? Like you weren't the one that just brought it up! I guess that sounds kind of…But really, he was…I'm sorry; I don't mean to keep talking about Flip. It's just that I don't know a lot of people these days."

Wayne gulped down half a glass of wine. "No…no, that does tell me more about you," he said, looking ridiculous with little purple stains curling up at the corners of his mouth. At the moment, Second Sight's contrast enhancement was not his friend. "But, um, you never did say what you do for a living."

"Oh, that." Laila took a sip of her own wine. "I work for

Triclave International. I'm in QA."

"Triclave, that's…yeah, that's right; you guys put out Second Sight! I'm a big fan."

Laila paused for another couple of sips. "So you, uh…you wear the lenses?"

"Well, no, I…can't really afford them right now," Wayne admitted. "But I use the drops every day. Never felt better!"

Ah yes, the drops. The natural next step in Second Sight's evolution. They weren't exactly *required*; you could still use plain old low-tech contact solution. But if you sustained any sort of injury while operating Second Sight without strict adherence to the manufacturer's instructions for use, then of course Triclave couldn't be held liable.

For example, if your nervous system reacted badly to extreme visual feedback and you found yourself having a panic attack in heavy freeway traffic, then you'd better hope you had enough Second Sight nanites in your bloodstream to detect the problem and shut off your lenses before things got out of hand. Then there were all the users with undiagnosed epilepsy. If you might be susceptible to seizures, you didn't want to find out the hard way. Better to self-administer your daily dose of nanotech and trust that your friends at Triclave International had your best interest at heart.

As an added bonus, Second Sight SmartDrops had been clinically proven to prolong focus and increase mental dexterity by up to thirty-three percent. *So you have people like this clown— no, that's not fair; he seems very nice—squirting tiny robots into their eyes hoping the little guys will build enough new synaptic connections to turn them into some kind of a genius? Well, it doesn't take a genius to recognize a con when you see it. Forget privacy; forget autonomy. You're going to hand over the keys to your one and only mortal vessel, and you're expected to* pay *for the privilege?!*

"…so it's really win-win." Wayne had been talking all this time, while Laila only stared at his high-contrast wine-stain mustache. She couldn't decide whether it was more Salvador

Dalí or Cesar Romero. Maybe if Dalí wore the Joker makeup. *Yeah, that would have been something to see.* "Laila?" Wayne was apparently finished talking and waiting on some kind of response.

"Right," Laila ventured. "Right…If only we'd had SmartDrops a few years ago…Flip might have noticed that van coming, and I'd be a married woman right now!" *Where did that come from?*

Wayne checked his phone. Laila finished her wine.

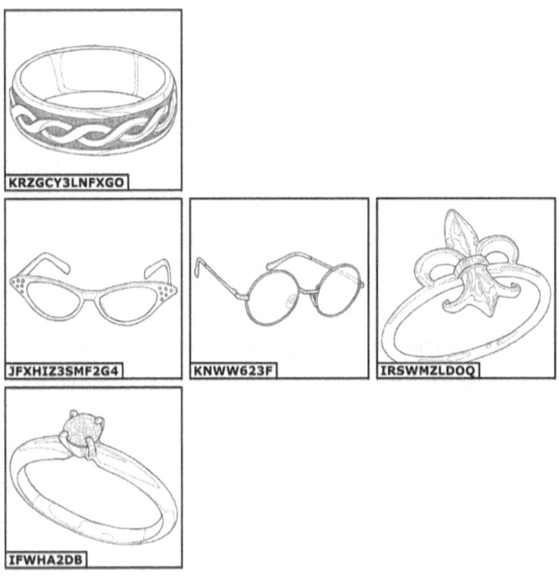

5. DEFECT

LAILA DIDN'T GET HOME THAT NIGHT UNTIL THE SMALL hours of the morning. This wasn't because of her date with Wayne Park though, not directly. After they'd split the check and gone their separate ways, Laila found she wasn't ready to be alone just yet. She drove awhile and ended up at the Twin Moons Mall.

As far as malls went, the atmosphere of Twin Moons was relatively mellow and low-key. It was something of a stylistic experiment, pushing the time-tested vaporwave aesthetic more toward stained glass and dark wood. This uncanny fusion had apparently missed the mark with customers, leaving half the stores out of business and the whole place feeling like a ghost town. But that suited Laila just fine. All she wanted was a safe place to walk.

Sometimes taking the right-hand path and sometimes the left, Laila walked the length of the second floor many times over, losing herself in an audiobook of *A Lens Faintly,* a classic by Thomas K. Blick. She had everything she needed: entertainment, exercise, vending machines, and enough security camera coverage to ward off all but the most brazen criminals.

Then out of nowhere came the strangest sensation. From the corner of her eye, Laila glimpsed what she took to be her own shadow keeping pace with her on the opposite walkway, across the gap in the floor. *That's not possible,* she thought with a shudder. *It's just another shopper.* But when she glanced discreetly over, it really was only a disembodied shadow, a faint person-shaped depression in the light. When she looked directly at it, the specter faded quickly out of existence. Then for a few seconds afterward, she could almost see the whole mall full of phantom shoppers, just walking back and forth like she had been.

She paused her book and noticed Elvis Presley's "Suspicious Minds" playing over the loudspeaker. The place was empty.

Did that just happen? No, that had to be my eyes playing tricks on me. Or my lenses. Laila tried to put the whole experience down to a combination of fatigue and boredom, but the sight had been too unnerving to brush off so easily. After a few minutes of searching around for unusual shadows, she told herself it had been a fluke, probably some transient glitch in Second Sight.

Or maybe the mall was haunted. The idea was laughable, but it caught Laila off guard, and a prickly wave rose up the back of her neck. She removed her lenses, and the Twin Moons Mall descended into drab, depressing reality. It was time to go home.

The next morning, she had the urge to ask around at work and see if anyone there had ever had a similar experience, but she didn't dare admit to what she'd seen—not until she was sure it had come from the lenses and not her own unsteady imagination. She decided to go SIA-free for a while. If she had another strange experience entirely on her own, then she'd know she was hallucinating, and she'd have the good sense to keep quiet about it.

She almost made it through an entire day this way, but sure enough, Levi Ferris stopped by her desk with a friendly reminder that ongoing participation in their flagship product was in no way optional. "We've got to eat our own dog food, you know? If our own team members don't believe in Second Sight, then how can we ask the rest of the world to put their faith in us?"

Laila got the message loud and clear: *Keep your lenses in or find another job.*

It wasn't until the following week that Laila got some external corroboration of her experience. She was trying out a new cafe—and trying not to admit to herself that she was really just avoiding Wayne—when a news report on one of the muted TVs caught her eye. It was right there in the closed captioning: "Following a recent firmware update, many Second Sight users have begun reporting unexplainable visions of shadowy human figures. These anomalies are usually short-lived, lasting only a few seconds, but some have been reported to persist for up to five minutes."

Endless debate ensued as to the nature of these anomalies— or "ghosts," as they came to be called. The most widely accepted theory, soon presented as scientific consensus, held that they were hyperdimensional entities, previously undetected but always physically present nonetheless.

As one talking head put it, "They're not human, but they're not exactly *alien* either. They've probably been with us from the beginning; we just haven't had a reliable means of detecting them until now. There might be any number of these ghosts just walking around, minding their own business, and we'd never know it because our perception is limited to this three-dimensional plane. Picture our known universe as a very thin sheet of paper." He waved a blank sheet around with his left hand and twirled his right index finger randomly. Then he brought his finger to the paper and pinned it down on his desk. "We're not the ones in control here. How could we be? We can't even see beyond the thickness of one sheet."

So that's it, huh? Ghosts are real; they're just not…ghosts. Laila found this theory a little hard to swallow. What about the simple explanation that there was something wrong with Second Sight? It might be malfunctioning, showing afterimages or glitchy predictive programming. Triclave's technology was cutting edge, but was it really so groundbreaking as to reveal these hidden people for the first time in human history? These ghosts or angels or demons or aliens or whatever they were…All this time, all we needed was the right contact lens?

It would seem so, yes.

The months that followed saw a nonstop flood of supporting evidence from all corners of the scientific world. Ghost hunting—complete with EMF meters and EVP recorders—became the new prestige hobby of America's youth and was unironically embraced by the same self-satisfied cognoscenti who continued to scoff at UFOs and Bigfoot and religion in all its forms. A handful of stubborn contrarians still questioned the official explanation, but they were routinely mocked and ridiculed by the masses. These ghost-denying skeptics were the new tinfoil underclass.

The physical existence of hyperdimensional ghosts became even harder to refute when people started dying—or more accurately, when a tentative link was established between ghost hunting and a rise in heart attacks. The message was the same, no matter the channel: "Avoid physical contact with any and all spectral anomalies. Preliminary reports indicate a greater-than-chance likelihood of concomitant disruption in cardiac function."

It was all very convincing. But there was a nagging voice in Laila's head that still didn't buy it. *That's just too good for business. Wear Second Sight at all times, or you may just drop dead.* A wry laugh escaped her throat.

"What's funny?" asked Neil, looking for the answer on Laila's computer screen.

"Oh, it's just…business is booming, you know? And I'm still not sure the damn things are safe."

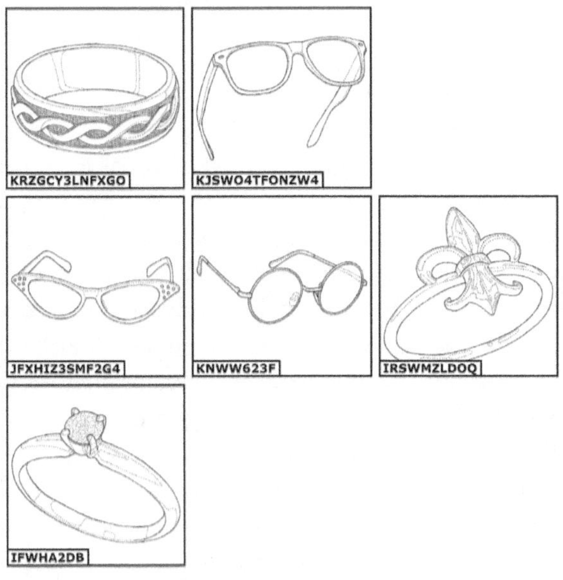

6. Regression

"LISTEN, NOBODY'S SAYING SMARTLENSES DON'T WORK. They're great. I know that better than anybody; believe me. But these ghosts they're giving us…I mean, come on. It's all a sham. Really, nobody knows this better than me. This kind of thing… It's show business, just like pro wrestling. You've got to give the audience a bad guy. Like these ghosts giving people heart attacks. People get scared; they have heart attacks. Get over it! If you're scared of ghosts, don't wear the lenses. Throw 'em out. I guarantee you'll be fine."

Laila closed the video in disgust. *How could anybody seriously be considering this guy for president?* Bill "Dumptruck" Dozier. Thirty years ago, he'd been a professional wrestler. Then when his popularity started to fade, he'd slyly transitioned into a perennial media personality. His abrasive, over-the-top style had earned him a loyal fan base, despite—or perhaps because of—the many scandals that dogged him throughout his career. He was a tax cheat, a philanderer, a bigot, a bully...pretty much everything you might expect from a guy named Dumptruck. And now he wanted to be president.

He knows better than anybody, huh? Right, what would I know? I'm just— On the rightmost edge of Laila's vision, a shadow passed through the hallway to her bedroom. Reflexively, she called out for her cat Martha. But of course, Martha couldn't have cast a shadow like that. *A ghost.* Despite their prominence in the news lately, Laila hadn't seen any ghosts since that night in the mall. She'd begun to lose faith in her own senses.

Without more than a moment's hesitation, she ran after the apparition, hoping to catch sight of it again before it faded. The bedroom looked the same as always. She checked under the bed and then peered into her closet. Nothing in there, except...Yes, there *was* something. Just inside the doorway, a faint silhouette sat with its back against the wall, hugging its knees to its chest. It looked so natural sitting there, just as Laila herself had done many times before, weeping in the dark. It looked right at home, not like any "hyperdimensional entity" she could picture. She'd sooner believe it was...

"Flip?" Her voice wavered as she tried again, a little louder this time: "*Flip?*"

There was no reaction from the shadowy figure. It didn't seem to hear her. Maybe there was another world where *Laila* was the silent shadow and this ghost was just an ordinary person living their life. And if that were the case, then why couldn't this other person be Flip? In that alternate world, it might have been Laila who died on impact and Flip who woke up a week later in a hospital bed.

On impulse, Laila reached out a hand to caress the side of Flip's face. But as soon as her fingers passed into darkness, a violent panic seized her and she pulled back involuntarily, like she'd just touched an electric fence. The figure remained motionless, completely unaffected.

As her heart rate began to slow, gradually returning to normal, Laila remembered Dumptruck Dozier's glib advice: "Don't wear the lenses." This triggered an unwelcome thought: *I can test that.* Occupational hazard. *Still,* she considered, *it might be worth it just to prove that smug asshole wrong.* Her reaction to the ghost had *not* been fear; it was something physical. That thing was real. She'd really touched it.

Still watching the ghost to make sure it didn't go anywhere, Laila pulled out her phone and disabled Second Sight. As soon as the lenses deactivated, she realized she hadn't turned on the bedroom lights. She probably hadn't used them in days. You get used to night vision. Hurriedly, she flipped the switch for the closet and saw that the ghost had indeed faded into obscurity. If Mr. Dozier was correct, then what she couldn't see couldn't hurt her, and there'd be no harm in reaching out to touch that empty space where— *Zzzap!*

There was that same buzzing panic again. Laila's heart fluttered in her chest with disconcerting irregularity. She wanted to say that settled the matter, but there was one more test she really couldn't ignore: She'd have to actually take her lenses out and try to touch the thing one more time totally disconnected from the system.

As quickly as she could manage, Laila pulled both lenses out of her eyes and once more reached toward that empty space where the ghost had been. Her hand trembled as she edged it closer, expecting a shock at any moment. But this time, there was nothing—no sensation at all. She fumbled to get her lenses back in and then blinked five times to start them up. No ghost. It must have already faded away when she'd reached for it the last time.

Unless…maybe it *was* all Second Sight. Was it somehow the lenses causing those sudden fits of panic? Had taking them out actually made the ghost go away, or was that just a coincidence? Or had there never been any ghost in the first place, just some kind of a hoax put on by Second Sight to sell more units? In one version of events, Second Sight was saving people. In another, it was killing them.

Laila felt like she'd been punched in the stomach. All the air was expelled from her lungs as she fell to the ground in a sobbing, aching heap. This was too much to process all at once. Flip was really, truly gone from this world. No more chasing at shadows. It looked like her company was callously killing its customers, feeding off an unlucky few in order to gather many more into the fold. And her government was no better. In a total surveillance state, complicity is much more likely than ignorance.

So what did that make Dumptruck Dozier? Some kind of hero of the people? Hell no. He was a straw man in a suit, a walking false flag. Ninety percent of everything he said was crap, and the remaining ten percent was sprinkled in there just to rub his stink on it. The question of whether he himself actually believed the things he said was irrelevant. He was a puppet in a long line of puppets. He played his part just as his so-called opponents were playing theirs.

What a depressing thought: *The real game isn't between the two teams on the field. It's between the spellbound fans and the sponsors finding new ways to empty their pockets*

7. COMPATIBILITY

LAILA WAS AWAKE NOW—TRULY AWAKE TO THE PITIFUL reality of her situation—but she had no idea what to do about it. It felt as if the world had suddenly revealed itself to be a dream. She knew that she was free to do whatever she wanted, but she didn't dare. Real or not, she had to go on living in this dream world day after day.

Neil turned his chair toward Laila and asked, "You going to the happy outing tonight?" His tone was casual, but Second Sight's thermal view made his nervous energy painfully obvious. Ever since Laila had stopped wearing her engagement ring—as if she'd had some choice in the matter—Neil had begun treating her differently. It felt like he was gearing up to ask her out, but this was the closest he'd come so far.

Laila answered in as neutral a tone as she could manage: "Sure, I'll make an appearance."

Of course she was going. When Triclave brass flew in from Fremont for their quarterly schmooze-fest, you had to play along. Besides, it was free booze. Appetizers too. She wasn't too proud to beg for scraps at the Triclave table—not on *her* budget. She made a decent salary, but most of that went to paying interest on her debts. Still, she was lucky to have a job at all. She had to keep reminding herself of that. She didn't feel lucky.

This particular "happy outing" got started around three in the afternoon. The original design of this "team-building event," as it was called, had taken advantage of happy hour discounts at the local bars. But over the years, it had grown beyond such insipid budgetary concerns. Each outing seemed to start a little earlier and end a little later than its predecessors. Once the revelry began to die down at the first location, the larger group typically fractured into a handful of smaller cliques, each headed by a manager or team lead with a corporate expense account.

As Laila saw it, there were a few separate forces driving these events. On the most obvious level, everyone enjoyed the free food and drinks. More than that though, they enjoyed making Triclave pay for it. No one likes putting a cash value on their own freedom, selling their soul two weeks at a time. But every one of them had done just that, and they resented the company for it.

So why was upper management okay with all of this? Why would they set aside such a large budget just to get their employees drunk every couple of months? Laila's theory was that when people drank, they talked. True feelings came out, secret relationships, hidden plans…useful things to know when it came time for restructuring and "right-sizing."

Contemplating the inner workings of Triclave International with no small amount of bitterness and self-loathing, Laila drained her glass of Armagnac and quickly ordered a Don Julio to take its place. "Actually, could you put a couple of cherries in that? And a little slice of orange? Thanks."

It was 20:12 in the evening, and the sun had finally gone

down. The outdoor seating at Arcadia Bar and Grille was made for nights like this. Cool and breezy. Excellent view of the waterway. Laila wondered what it would be like to actually visit Arcadia on her own dime. It seemed like a nice enough place to sit and while away a Friday evening, if one were so inclined. *I'd probably need to gather up a few friends, though, or the drinking would get lonely fast.* And that would be easier said than done. Most of her friends were really more *Flip's* friends, and she hadn't bothered to keep in touch following his death. In any case, the obscene prices would almost certainly diminish her enjoyment. No, this place was for happy outings only.

A few of the less committed Second Sight employees had already excused themselves and headed home for the night. The remainder of the group was quietly preparing itself for fragmentation.

"So…where are we headed for round two?" Laila asked no one in particular.

Neil seized on this as if she'd addressed him directly. "You want to head someplace quieter?" he asked.

"Quieter, louder…Anyplace is good as long as I don't get stuck with the bill."

"You drive a hard bargain, Laila," said Neil with a smirk. "Come on. I know a place."

At this point, Laila's head was swimming from hours of free drinks. She got up and stumbled through the patio gate without once turning back to see that nobody else had risen to join them—no manager with a company card, only her and Neil. He gripped her arm proprietorially as they climbed into an autocab, and before Laila could even think to ask where they were going, they'd arrived at their destination.

The place was called Jacob's Ladder, and it was in no way quieter than Arcadia. Neil had apparently taken Laila at her word that she didn't care. Besides the music, a bass-heavy electronic mangling of "Für Elise," the first thing that struck her about this establishment was its apparent lack of any sort of dress code. *Although,* she thought, *it hardly matters these days. Most of these people are probably wearing lenses with unauth bodyscan filters anyway.* This was definitely more of a dance club than a restaurant or bar, an odd choice for a company outing even if it was round two.

"Hey, I didn't see…" Laila shouted over the music. "Who else is coming?"

"Here?" Neil looked around sheepishly. "It's just us tonight."

"Oh no," Laila said as the realization finally dawned on her. "You're trying to take me out, aren't you? Like this is some kind of date."

Neil's face fell, and then his expression hardened into something hateful. "Well, I *thought* that you…Why'd you get in the cab with me if you're just gonna—"

"What did you think was gonna happen?"

"Never mind; forget it. Just find your own way home. I've got better things to do than babysit a drunk."

Laila was in no mood to be dismissed like that. Not tonight. "Listen, you—you absolute *waste* of human life. You may walk and talk and breathe like me…eat and sleep and do all the other things…but we are *not* the same."

"Wow, you really are hammered. Maybe you should just—"

"Where do you go at night, huh? When you sleep? Do you dream? Are you even *real?* Or is this all there is for you?" She waved a hand around to indicate the club, its patrons, and the rest of the waking world. "What's the *point* of you?"

Neil had no answer. He just stood there looking puzzled and irritated.

"If you think this is life," Laila continued, "if you think all this is gonna add up to something…then I don't—I don't even know what to tell you."

Now Neil's smug self-assurance returned in force. "You're out of your mind. But you are not my problem. Sleep it off. I'll see you Monday."

On impulse, Laila pulled out both of her Second Sight lenses and tossed them down onto the floor of Jacob's Ladder. "Nah…" she said. "You're not gonna see me Monday. I'm out. Tell Levi I quit. Or actually…He's gonna see this, right? He's watching?" Laila stepped closer to Neil, put her hands on his shoulders, and looked right into his eyes. "I quit, Levi! *Non serviam.* I'm done being part of this thing. I'd rather be nothing at all."

8. execution

IT WAS DARK OUTSIDE. LAILA HAD BEEN USING SECOND Sight for so long, she'd forgotten how dark it got after sundown. Or maybe the city had been cutting back on street lights since most of its taxpayers wore smartlenses anyway. Never mind the eighty percent of the population who fell below the poverty line. They couldn't afford to complain and risk losing their dole. *Don't bite the hand that feeds you,* as the saying went. *Unless it's also holding the key to your cage. That might actually be worth it. Tough call.*

Laila pulled out her phone to get her bearings. It was only half past nine. It felt later than that. She was a little over two miles from home. Totally walkable in daylight, but maybe not such a good idea at night. *But if I get a cab right now, I might be sick in it.* She decided to try and sober up a little by walking back and forth.

From the corner of her eye, Laila noticed a dark figure across the street keeping pace with her. She whipped her head around in a panic, expecting to see it vanish like the one in the Twin Moons Mall. But this time, she wasn't wearing Second Sight. *Could it be real?* She forced her eyes to focus on the shadowy blur. It was just an ordinary old man. He did bear more than a passing resemblance to Elvis Presley, but…*No, that's probably nothing. Probably.* Laila burst out laughing and started back on her way.

"Wait! Stop!" called a shrill voice behind her. It was a pudgy little woman carrying a giant shopping bag. "You almost walked into a ghost," she said. "Are you not wearing your lenses?"

"Second Sight is a scam," Laila snapped back at her. "There are no ghosts! It's all in the lenses. They show you shadows, and then they give you a shock just to keep you scared. Well, I'm not falling for it, not any more."

"Oh great, a Dumptrucker," muttered the woman, clutching her bag a little tighter.

"What? No, I'm not…Look, I'll prove it! If you take the lenses out, they can't hurt you. Where's the ghost? Here?" Laila took a few steps forward, waving her hands in front of her. And then, unmistakably, she felt it.

She couldn't breathe. Her shoulders tensed up. There was a burning pressure deep in her chest. Everything was spinning, making her so dizzy she had to sit down right there on the sidewalk. *Now I know I'm going to be sick,* she thought. But the cool concrete felt so nice on her cheek as she laid down her throbbing head. *Maybe I just need to rest a minute.*

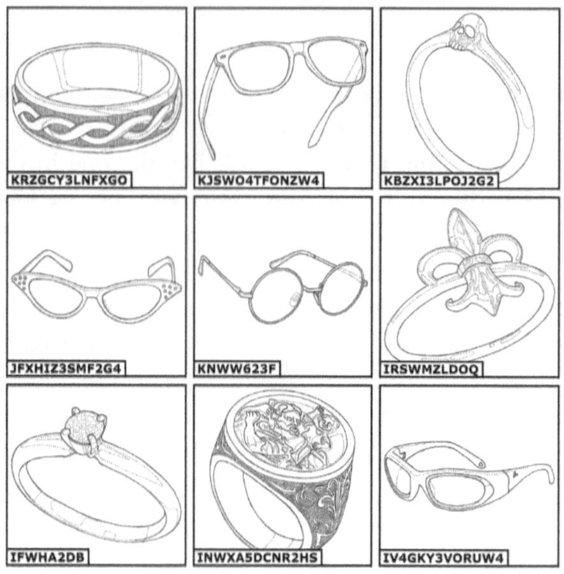

9. POSTMORTEM

WHERE HAD THE MORNING GONE? NO MATTER HOW EARLY Laila set her alarm, she always seemed to be running late for work. It was time to leave, and she hadn't even thought about breakfast. The night before, her fiancé Flip had cooked and packed away some leftovers, so that was covered at least. Lasagna. Not bad. It certainly beat the cafeteria at Livetrac headquarters.

Laila threw the leftovers into an old grocery bag with a granola bar and a jumbo can of herbal energy drink. As she shut the fridge, a shadowy figure caught her attention from the corner of her eye. She was gripped by an unreasoning dread that raised a lump in her throat and stopped her breathing. An instant later, the figure revealed itself to be only a shadow across the floor. But this was a *moving* shadow—a writhing, seething mass of…ants?

"Flip!" she called out. "We've got ants in the kitchen."

"Ugh, *again?*" Flip stumbled down the hall in nothing but

boxer shorts, rubbing his forehead with one palm. "All right, I'll—I'll figure it out." He ran both hands back through an unruly mane of curls and flyaways. Even his sideburns stuck out in all directions. At least he didn't have a beard. That would have been entirely too much mountain man for Laila.

"Don't you have an interview today?" she asked.

Flip seemed to think about it. "Yeah. Yeah, that's at eleven."

"Hm," Laila replied, giving in to her critical side. "Is there enough time to squeeze in a haircut?"

"I thought you wanted me to deal with these ants," Flip teased. "Anyway, no, there's no extra time. Or money."

"We definitely have enough money for you to get a haircut. It's an investment. At least get rid of those giant Elvis sideburns."

"But they make me look like Elvis!" Flip whined jokingly, brushing them down with his fingertips.

Laila opened the apartment door, edging out even as she spoke. "A little. But not the version of Elvis you're thinking of."

Flip ran at her like a mad bull, and for just a moment Laila was actually afraid. He was twice her size and not particularly graceful. But then he stopped just short of her, squeezed her up in a bear hug, and gave her a solid kiss, apparently unashamed to be outside in his underwear. "I'll miss you," he said, releasing her back into the world.

"Same," she replied. "Good luck today."

"Thanks. You too."

Laila's drive downtown started like every other morning, but once she hit the freeway, the other cars took on a terrifying new aspect. They seemed to skitter past her like living creatures. Their movements were purposeful, organic, just the slightest bit unsteady. It was as if instead of rubber tires, each wheel comprised thousands of tiny insectoid limbs, all black and chitinous with cruel hooked claws for feet.

Laila could picture the flow of traffic all around her. From above, she watched the cars move along in streams like all those ants on her kitchen floor. What had they been looking for anyway? A crumb here, a speck of sugar there? The vast stockpiles of food in the pantry and fridge remained untouched. For that matter, what kept all these cars returning to the city day after day? A little money, a little entertainment? Surface operations like Livetrac kept the ants fighting over crumbs while the obscene fortunes of a shadowy elite were counted not in dollars but in lives.

The thought was nothing new, of course. It was common knowledge, though commonly ignored. Laila was only able to comfortably acknowledge the idea now because she was…what? Woolgathering? Daydreaming? No, something much deeper than that. How was she able to view all those tiny vehicles from above? She could see them all so clearly now, even the large black van that was currently pushing her own economy coupe into the guardrail of an overpass. And there it went breaking through, falling…Her car tumbled sidelong into the stream of traffic below. It was this second collision that took her life.

At least, that was the way Laila remembered it. All of that was so distant now, like another world. More than that, it seemed unreal, imagined—like a story she'd been told to help explain her fragmented condition, why she always felt so disconnected from the world around her.

And what a strange world it was. Compared to those dull memories of her old apartment and morning commute, this new world flashed and pulsed with radiant consciousness. There was nothing in it that was not alive—nothing that was not *Laila,* in fact. It was uncanny to be both figure and ground, actor and audience. But the feeling soon passed, and Laila returned to herself with no recollection of the universe she had been.

Now she saw Flip on his laptop in an unassigned cubicle, the type generously termed a "breakout room" by ValiCert Systems and other like-minded corporate entities. Flip didn't look like himself. Too clean cut. No sideburns. A blonde woman approached the cubicle, speaking in that chipper, authoritative tone that immediately revealed her to be a human resources manager. Behind her trailed a group of overdressed new hires hanging on her every forcefully projected word.

"Here we have Flip Foster, one of our QA specialists. Could you give us an idea what you do here, Flip?"

Flip raised a hand and nodded awkwardly. "Okay, well, first off, this isn't my real desk here. I actually have a corner office with big windows and a view of the park...-*ing lot.*" A couple of people laughed politely. "At home. I work from home." No reaction from the group this time. This was painful to watch. "I only come here for the coffee! Anyway…"

Before he could actually make his way to the question posed by the HR tour guide, Flip caught sight of Laila, and everyone else faded into the background. One moment they were human beings with their own distinct minds and perceptions and personalities, and the next they were scenery—all but invisible. *If a shift in Flip's attention can do that,* Laila marveled, *then whose dream is it really?*

Without a word, the two of them stepped toward each other and embraced tightly. Laila leaned her head on Flip's chest while he breathed in the scent of her hair. The world around them rippled and buckled, threatening to disintegrate entirely.

"I'm mad at you," Laila said through streaming tears.

"Why?"

"I liked the Elvis sideburns."

Flip laughed, but Laila felt a warm teardrop hit the top of her head. There was a force at work here that they both knew was best left unacknowledged. They had to try and appreciate their time together without putting too much thought into *why* it was so precious, how it could evaporate at any moment and leave them marooned once more in their separate threads of reality.

A chill wind blew through the office, and the walls of Flip's cubicle rattled like cardboard. The tour group had disappeared entirely now; even Laila's memory of them was fading.

"Sorry," Flip said, breaking contact with Laila. "We can't keep—you know, if you fall asleep, then you'll—we've got to pay more attention to *here and now,* this situation we're in." Even as he said this, fine details began to creep back into their surroundings, replacing a sort of muddy nothing that Laila hadn't noticed until it was already ebbing away like a clearing fog.

Suddenly, a familiar voice called from down the hall: "Flip! Come take a look at this."

Gripping Laila's hand tightly and glancing frequently back at her in apology, Flip followed the voice to a room stacked floor to ceiling with cardboard boxes. There in a far corner was Neil Conrad. He was sitting on a box that had an image of an office chair on it. Too lazy to unpack the box and put the chair together, apparently.

Typical Neil, she thought. Then she wondered where the idea had come from—and how she even knew this guy's name. She was certain she'd never met him before, but there was another part of her that wasn't certain of anything.

Neil leaned forward and tapped on a computer box that had been stood up in imitation of a screen. "We've got a bug in here. I can hear it scratching around." He glanced over at Laila and nodded, failing to show any sort of recognition.

Flip walked over and put his ear to the computer box, furrowing his brow. "Sounds like more than one."

Laila suddenly felt awkward, out of place. With Flip's attention elsewhere, she was essentially alone in an unfamiliar office with no clue how she'd gotten there. The name "ValiCert" sounded familiar, but she couldn't quite place it.

Flip and Neil took no notice as she walked over to them. Their attention was fixed on a faint scratching sound coming from within the box. Flip traced a path on its surface with his finger, presumably following the sound of the bug. Then holding his finger on one particular spot, he took a wooden pencil from Neil and cautiously held its sharpened tip against the spot. With his other hand, he drew back an open palm and slammed it into the pencil, embedding it deeply in the cardboard.

"Did you get it?" Neil asked hopefully.

As if in answer, something inside the box pushed the pencil slowly back out. It fell to the floor with a light clatter. For a moment, this was the only sound in the universe. And then through the hole dribbled a bit of dark liquid, like motor oil or molasses, followed by what looked like a tiny mechanical spider or crab. First one, then another, then two more at once…Each of these "bugs" made the hole just a bit wider with its scraping claws until they were pouring out by the dozen, leaving trails of the sticky black liquid behind them.

Neil shrieked in panic, and the sound seemed to draw the creatures toward him. Behaving as a single hive organism, the mass of tiny robotic bugs swarmed over every inch of him, digging under his skin and flooding into his open mouth.

Flip stepped back, just staring in horrified disbelief. Laila grabbed him by the arm and pulled him through the nearest door, slamming it shut behind them. This did little good, however. The bugs were small enough to slip under the door without much trouble. Laila knew there was no true hope of escape, but she kept running all the same. The alternative was unthinkable.

After several turns through what felt like a city-sized maze, Flip looked back and saw what he and Laila had already known: Hallway after empty hallway, the bugs kept right on coming, trailing behind them like skittering, undulating shadows. Laila needed no visual confirmation herself. She'd already imagined the scene with such vivid clarity that it was hard to tell where imagination ended and reality began.

"You've got to wake up!" Flip rasped in a sort of whispered yell. "This is all you! I can't…" He trailed off as the window up ahead caught his eye.

Laila knew instantly what he was thinking. *Through the window?!* She trusted Flip, but not quite enough for that. Before she could object, though, Flip was already crouching behind her and using their combined momentum to push her through the glass.

But it wasn't glass. It was cellophane.

Passing through this transparent film and into the chill night air, Laila registered another welcome surprise: The outside walls didn't go straight down but were instead slanted at a forty-five-degree angle. The building was actually a pyramid! And mercifully, instead of bricks or concrete, the exterior was covered in flat squares of cardboard—thousands of them as far as she could see. As she hurtled down the slope, Laila managed to grab onto one of these cardboard sheets and keep it under her, using it as a makeshift sled. This didn't last long, however, as she soon reached the ground and tumbled to a skidding halt in the cool, damp grass.

Lying there on her back, staring up at the stars, she now heard a faint skittering noise that made her blood run cold. It seemed the bugs had caught up with her already. She clenched her eyes shut, hoping only for a swift end to her suffering.

But it didn't come. Now that she'd stopped moving, the bugs could take their time. Laila saw six of the creatures make their approach. They'd grown much taller now, almost like little people. They stood above her all in a row, staring down with their unblinking insectoid eyes, those expressionless metal faces…Or were they just masks?

"Get out of here!" Laila growled, barely recognizing the voice as her own.

The blue one started to cry.

Hesitantly, the yellow one held up a paper bag and said, "Trick or treat?" Its mouth didn't move, but the voice sounded perfectly human—like a child.

Through a fog of uncanny revulsion, Laila managed to ask, "What *are* you?"

"Power Patrol!" replied the creatures, as if that were supposed to mean something.

"Bugs," Laila muttered, still reeling from the dream. "It's them damn bugs. Under my skin. In my blood!" She sat up and looked around. Yancy Park. Home.

At this point, a ponytailed woman with an uneasy smile hurried up to usher the children away. "Tommy? Come here. It's okay." She hugged the boy in blue and comforted him a moment before turning to Laila. "I'm so sorry. Were they bothering you?" She tilted her head, raised her eyebrows, and pressed her lips tightly together. In the years following Laila's unceremonious break with Second Sight, she'd seen this pitying expression too many times to count.

Laila rubbed the bridge of her nose and frowned. "Nah, it's green,"

"I'm so sorry," the woman repeated. "I don't have any cash on me. Do you take CredShare?"

"You kidding me right now? I ain't selling nothing."

"Oh, I didn't mean…No, I'm sorry; I just wanted to—"

"Wait a minute," Laila broke in. "You see ghosts? You got Second Sight?"

"Well…*yeah,*" answered the woman, as if Laila had just asked if she wore shoes or brushed her teeth in the morning.

No, that ain't gonna work, Laila decided. She looked around and yelled out, "Maggie!" The ponytailed woman, visibly startled, took this as her cue to back off, quietly ushering the Power Patrol away with her. Laila's understanding of Second Sight's role in her heart attack all those years ago had finally clicked into place. "Maggie, where you at?" She scrambled to her feet and began searching for her friend. *I gotta be more careful,* she told herself. *Gotta stay away from them wumps with their lenses. And the drops. Never should have put that dreck into my body.* "Maggie!"

And then there was good old Maggie Moon strolling up the path, casual as anything. Maggie was Laila's one constant anchor in a sea of confusion. With that floral kimono jacket, her gray-streaked mass of natural coils, and that ever-billowing corncob pipe, she was impossible to miss. "What's the matter, girl?" she said between puffs. "What do you need?"

"I need *you,*" answered Laila. "Just—just tell me what's up, will you?"

Maggie grinned knowingly and assumed that dreamy, far-off look she always wore when she was about to grace this mortal plane with a sampling of her hard-earned cosmic wisdom. "Well, I'll tell you what's up. The *light* is up." She raised a finger to the sky and then immediately thrust it downward. "The dark is down. Right? Same as ever. Least that's how most people tell it."

She paused here to puff on her pipe and consider how to proceed with the sermon.

"Them wumps up top, they wanna shine their light all over down here. Can't nobody hide for long, not really. But if you think about it...they're the ones with all the secrets, keeping all their dealings in the dark. We're already lit up down here! What more do they think we're hiding? Not much, I'll tell you. Scraps." On this last word, Maggie's conviction faltered; her mask slipped a little.

She didn't speak again for some time, so Laila took up the thread: "Secrets, yeah. They hoard up secrets like they do with money and land and everything else. I ain't got no more secrets *left*. Second Sight took the last of them."

"Say, Laila..." Maggie ventured. "I got a secret. You want in?" She didn't wait for a reply but continued in the next breath: "You know I used to roll wumps here and there before I got cleaned up?"

"Yeah. 'Here and there,' huh?"

"Well, the thing is...A lot of that stuff I took, I knew I couldn't sell it without catching heat, so...I got me a little treasure trove. You wanna see?"

Laila looked around, disbelieving what she'd heard. "You're gonna show me? So like...it'll be *our* secret?"

"Yeah, that's right. Nobody's got my back like you. Green?"

At this point, Laila found herself on the verge of tears, so she just nodded her assent and followed Maggie in silence. Deep in the heart of Yancy Park, beside an unnamed stream, beneath a concrete footbridge, there was a single loose brick. Maggie took a minute to work the thing free and then placed it carefully on the ground, as if the brick itself were more valuable than the trinkets it concealed—which in a way, it was. Hiding places were hard to come by.

In one careful, almost reverent motion, Maggie scooped up a handful of tangled jewelry from the secret cavity and then spread the items out across both of her palms to show Laila. It was difficult to see clearly in the shadow of the bridge, but the moon hung low in the sky, so the treasure glinted faintly.

"See anything you want?" asked Maggie in a whisper. "It's been so long…nobody's gonna be looking for this stuff no more."

Laila reached out and ran her fingers over the jewelry in Maggie's hands. A few necklaces, a wristwatch, several rings… One of them felt familiar. She held it up and watched the moonlight spill through its emerald inset.

"This one," Laila said simply, and slipped it on. It fit perfectly.

PART 3
KICKING THE HIVE

In which a group of students share a dream
And things are not so desperate as they seem

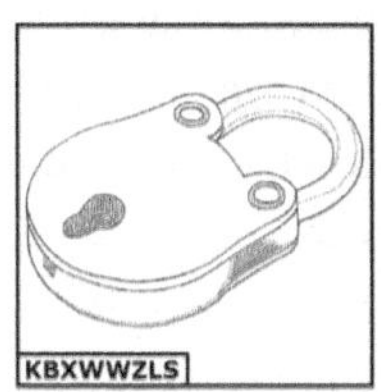

1. POKER

"YOU SERIOUSLY DON'T REMEMBER *ANYTHING*? NOTHING at all from the whole sim?" Levi Ferris paused a moment to accentuate his question and then continued dealing out the next hand of poker.

Neil Conrad picked up his next card as it fell, saying, "I told you, it's like a dream. I never remember my dreams."

Levi frowned inwardly, which only made his outward grin tighten. Hadn't anybody ever taught this wump to play poker? *Who picks up their cards one at a time?* "How do you expect to graduate if you can't recall a single lesson?"

"Who says I want to graduate?"

Fair point. "*How* about the rest of you?" Levi continued. "Lessons learned?" Levi looked at each face in turn as he dealt their cards face down in front of them. Only Violet Valdez met his gaze, raising her thoroughly pierced eyebrows in silent non-answer. Best not to begin with Violet. "Wayne? How about you?"

Wayne Park wore his usual "Why me?" expression, but he answered dutifully: "I…I remember I really liked the tech again. But then it all turned out kind of messed up. Again."

"I didn't like this last sim at all," said Flip Foster from behind his ridiculous mirrorshades. "I was dead for most of it, just bumming around as a ghost. *Again.*"

Levi had to laugh at this. "Well, I've got to say, that one's on *you.* You've got to do a better job keeping yourself alive!"

"I don't know what happened this last time, but the time before that, you—"

"Oh, come on!" Maggie Moon broke in. "Don't act so innocent. I *remember* the time before that."

That shut Flip up pretty quickly. He might have been looking over at Laila Duchamp, but it was hard to tell. No wonder he wore the shades.

A plump gray cat hopped up onto the table and walked casually across the ante chips. "Here, Martha," Maggie called in a much softer tone than she'd used on Flip, and the cat settled into her lap.

"Really though, why do we keep repeating the same mistakes?" asked Laila. "I feel like I learned…to be more assertive maybe? To break away from the crowd and make up my own mind."

"Careful," said Violet, picking up her cards. "Don't let on you've learned *too* much or Mr. Ferris might graduate you."

Neil snickered, and everyone else looked at Levi for a response.

"You'll all graduate when you're ready," he said. "I really don't have much control over that. I mean, I do what I can, but—"

"You do what you can to run me off the road!" Flip shouted. "Or have me shot in the head, or—"

"Come on, that's not fair," said Levi. "Inside the HiVE, I'm no more in control than the rest of you. I may have a little more practice, but we all create the sim together. I'm just the N-plus-one input, you know? A little older, a little wiser…"

Wayne laughed politely, while Violet let out a decidedly impolite "Ha!"

It really was true though. Levi was an instructor in name only. He was a grad student, which meant he was responsible for observing the progress of his undergrads and writing some kind of thesis about them, which honestly *nobody* was ever going to read. Why should they? It all came down to HiVE performance in the end. Statistics. Rankings. All the really important decisions were standardized and automated.

Once the Holoimmersive Virtual Environment was introduced into the university system, it served as a viable means to put the whole thing on autopilot. No more classes, no more faculty. Just sims over and over until the students eventually got it right. A lifetime of trial and error each and every night, all expenses paid and relatively safe from the 'demics that ravaged the waking world.

No wonder most students dreaded graduation. Entering the workforce was like one last long night with nothing after it but the terrifying certainty of death. This was the reason grad school was such a popular option. There was more work involved, but you still got the HiVE every night. Until your nine weeks were up. Then it was all over. Unless of course you qualified for the doctoral track, but that was exceedingly rare these days. Levi didn't hold out much hope for a career in academia.

No, his lives were numbered. Only twenty-two left, plus one waking life at the end.

"Look," Levi said, "I've got graduation hanging over my head too. Unless I can work a miracle and get at least half of you graduated by—" Violet raised her eyebrows again. Okay, maybe she had a point. "Anyway, it's late. I'm out after this hand. I'm ready to hit the HiVE."

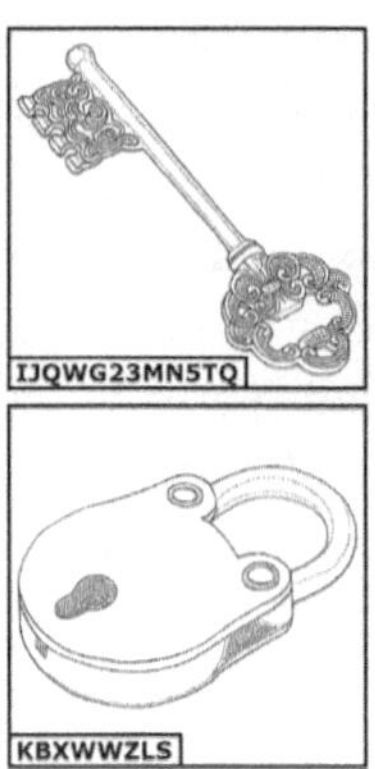

2. Backlog

"I'M SORRY, SIR," RATTLED MAGGIE'S VOICE OVER THE intercom. "No drivers available till Wednesday."

Wednesday?! Levi stewed. *If they only knew…they'd prioritize.* "Fine," he answered back. "I'll make the delivery myself. Not like *I'm* busy or anything."

Maggie made no reply. She just left Levi hanging, wondering whether his heavy sarcasm was too subtle for her.

"Where's the package?" he continued at last.

"Ground floor, bay twenty-three."

The elevator took its time going down. It was so sluggish that Levi suspected it might be about to give out entirely. *Why do they stick the execs on the top floors anyway?* "Top of the pyramid," Levi muttered, a sardonic grin on his lips.

Bay twenty-three was a storage locker, one of many, the size of a small garage. Levi used his keycard to gain entry and raised the roll-up door to reveal a single nondescript briefcase. It didn't look like much, but the dreck it contained was worth more than his annual salary. An ounce of dreck was quite literally worth its weight in gold.

Dreck: part drug, part nanotech, part biological material… all with the taste and appearance of blackstrap molasses. It represented the latest development in the ancient tradition of "dirty medicine," or *Dreckapotheke*. The full spectrum of dreck's applications had yet to be discovered, but suffice it to say a dreck trip was an eye-opening experience. In order to fund further research, Triclave United had resorted to selling small batches for distribution across the border. No judgment from Levi. Whatever paid the bills.

The briefcase was frayed and worn down at its edges, the security equivalent of driving an old piece of junk to avoid having your car stolen—which incidentally, Levi did. He carried the case out to his reserved parking spot in the adjoining garage and placed it carefully on the passenger seat of his dusty black hatchback. He considered rigging up the seatbelt around the thing but gave up after a few awkward tries. *Don't overthink it,* he told himself. *It's just like delivering a pizza.*

Levi drummed his fingers on his left wrist, entering the destination into his smartlenses. A translucent map appeared before his eyes, showing a stylized satellite view of the traffic in real time. His own car inched along in blue as possible obstacles (all the other cars in his vicinity) lit up in red. The map showed extensive bomb damage on I-10. He'd have to take Transmountain. "Okay, looks like we're taking the scenic route," he informed his precious cargo.

And for just an instant, he could have sworn the briefcase— or the dreck inside—actually *responded.* Not in words, of course, but with a feeling of recognition, of something like deja vu. The substance was *alive* in a sense, but intelligent? Psychic? *Wow, get a grip, man. Pizza, remember?*

As he wound around the mountain bends, climbing past the

desert foothills, ever farther from the concrete chaos of the city, he began to feel a certain satisfaction with himself and his life thus far. He really wasn't doing too badly. Pretty green, all things considered. *Must be the clean mountain air,* he thought, rolling his windows down to bask in the feeling. *Top of the pyramid.*

At this point, everything went into slow motion. You'd think that would have given Levi quicker reaction time or decision making, but no. That was all in slow motion too.

What Levi saw, what he really focused on, was those damn wrap-around mirrored sunglasses. They caught the sunlight in just the right way—the *wrong* way, really—and as he came around the bend, it looked like the sun was coming out from behind the rocks. Levi flinched and threw up his arm to block the light, but before he could course-correct, the kid on the motorcycle had already fallen into a hopeless skid trying to get back into his own lane.

And then, as Levi swerved to the left for some inexplicable reason, he felt the motorcycle crunch under his wheels—first the front and then the back—right along with that kid in those ridiculous mirrorshades.

It all seemed to happen so *slowly.* Levi couldn't get over how avoidable the whole thing was. *Get out of the way!* he screamed inside his head. *What are you thinking?!* But of course, the kid had no more time to avoid the collision than Levi did.

And once the damage had been done, Levi's car kept right on moving. As he'd rolled over the motorcycle, the jerk of his steering wheel had sent the car into a skid of its own. This was soon interrupted by a collision with a large boulder on the passenger side—finally causing the airbags to deploy—followed shortly thereafter by a swift loss of consciousness.

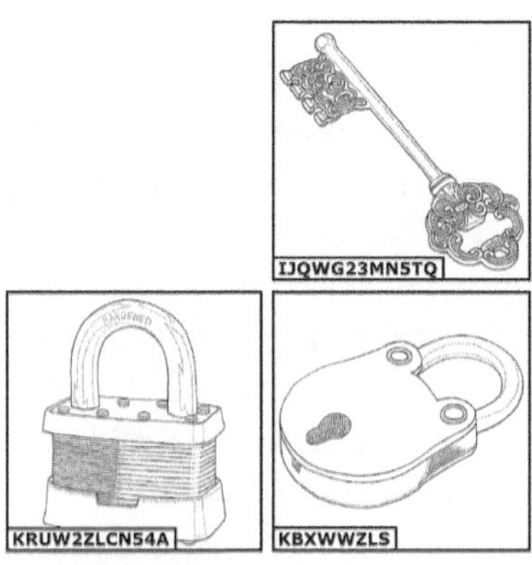

3. TIMEBOX

"FLIP! WHAT DO YOU HAVE IN YOUR MOUTH?" HIS MOTHER tried to look stern, but she was fighting back laughter. Even a toddler could see it.

"Nuffing," little Flip Foster said through a mouthful of chocolate. He was too young to imagine how ridiculous he looked.

"Nothing, huh?" It was his first girlfriend now, Maggie Moon. "No flowers or chocolate?"

"I didn't want you to think—" Flip started. "I mean…that's old-fashioned, right? Why didn't *you* get *me* flowers?"

Maggie rolled her eyes and turned toward the hospital bed. So many flowers surrounded it that you could hardly see the man lying there. Flip's grandpa was dying for sure. The room looked like the funeral had already started: tearful relatives crowded in, the old man laid out motionless on the bed, wall-to-wall flowers and balloons…The room smelled of antiseptic and decay. The only thing missing was a slideshow with cheesy uplifting music.

And there it was. *Ugh, why so much singing?* The music was definitely the worst part of church. Practically every week, Flip's family managed to be late to the Sunday service, but they were never quite late enough to miss the singing, unfortunately.

"And what's wrong with his singing?" asked his roommate Wayne. "I mean, really, who's a better singer than Nat King Cole?"

"It's not about that," Flip laughed. "Sure, the man can sing. It's just…Come on, he's corny as hell."

"Hell is other people," Neil said with a smirk, as if that would put an end to the debate.

"The hell it is!" Flip shot back. "Hell is separation from the Divine, and people…People are a manifestation of God— in God's image, you know—so Hell is…it's just being alone. Forever."

The room fell silent. No one had expected the class clown to get so serious, least of all Flip himself.

"Who said that?" Neil asked. "What's your source?"

Flip was tired of arguing. "*I* said it. Who else? There's no one else here…no one anywhere anymore."

And it was true. There was nothing left but memories. And they were all jumbled.

Everything went black. Quiet. Empty. For the millionth time, Flip revisited the moment of his death.

He hadn't seen the little black hatchback coming around the bend until it was already too late to avoid it. *What was it doing in my lane anyway?!* He'd actually drifted a little too far to the left, and the hatchback hadn't quite crossed the line at the time of impact. *But still, it was definitely going too fast.* That was true. *And besides, I had the sun in my eyes.* Flip's mirrorshades weren't really dark enough to help with that.

Skipping right over his grisly finale, Flip tried once again to push past the edge of his allotted time on Earth. He could usually watch the aftermath of the wreck for just about a minute or so before being pulled back into his personal history, his "timebox" as he'd come to think of it. He could look around in there to his heart's content, but not before his birth or after his death. His time in the world of the living had come to an end, it seemed.

Flip crouched down to look inside the overturned hatchback. The driver was hanging upside-down by his seatbelt, held in place by a deployed airbag. The man was apparently unconscious and covered in blood. *No, not blood.* It looked more like…*Molasses?*

Out of curiosity, Flip reached out to touch the man's chin, which was dripping with the stuff. But just before he made contact, the man's eyes opened wide, and he took in a ragged breath. It took Flip a moment to realize it, but the driver was actually looking right at him. He could *see* him. It had been so long that Flip had almost forgotten what that felt like.

"Hello?" Flip ventured.

The man only smiled, inky black stains on his teeth. He looked out of his mind, probably in shock from the accident. Or from seeing a ghost.

"Rough day, huh?" Flip couldn't help taunting the man who'd just taken his life. "Put yourself in my shoes."

And then, just before the universe pulled him back into his own personal slice of eternity, Flip realized something: He *knew* this guy. The driver was…his teacher? *Sort of.* It was Levi Ferris. *From college, from Triclave University!* And that sticky black mess all over him…that had to be dreck. Or at least some version of the drug he knew. *That's how we start. How we get ready for…class?*

It made no sense. Flip had never been to college. But he remembered *everything* now—so much more than a lifetime. And at the center of it all was Laila Duchamp. She was the one he was supposed to be with, not Maggie Moon. Maggie was… well, she was amazing, but that didn't really matter. That was never going to work because she and Flip didn't understand each other. They'd just make each other miserable, life after life. Laila was the one he needed. And now that he *knew*…

There were so many possibilities to explore. *And all the time in the world to do it.*

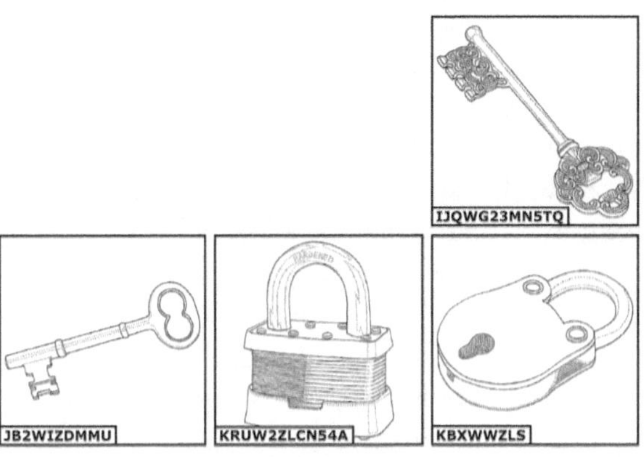

4. HUDDLE

A NOTIFICATION CAME UP IN MAGGIE MOON'S LENSES: "Levi Ferris has shared their location with you." She knew what that meant: "Come get me."

"You need me to pick you up?" she pinged back to be sure.

Maggie hurriedly finished her coffee while waiting for a response. She went right down to the last sip and then stopped. She always stopped before the last sip. It was still warm, and she knew there weren't any coffee grounds in it or anything, but it had lost its appeal nonetheless. *Dregs. No, thank you.*

"Yep," came Levi's first ping, followed soon after by: "Can't talk now. Delivery incomplete. Cancel it. Bigger fish."

Bigger than this delivery that couldn't wait till Wednesday? Maggie imagined a few possibilities, and none of them sat well with her.

From her burner phone, she sent their distributor a brief prearranged cancellation message: "Non serviam."

In a moment, a generic confirmation came back: "Ad majorem Dei gloriam."

Even though the pings were heavily encrypted, communication was kept strictly formulaic so that you'd have to already know what was being discussed in order to understand anything. Dreck was too novel to be specifically forbidden as a controlled substance, but it did fall under the more general regulations of the FDA. So while they wouldn't have the DEA to contend with in the event of discovery, the FBI, CIA, NSA, and SIA could still get involved, and that was just the tip of a very large, well-funded iceberg.

Doing her best not to panic, Maggie got her things together to go pick up Levi. On her way out, she stuck her head into Neil Conrad's office. "Hey, Neil…"

He raised a finger and then continued typing for another thirty seconds or so. Just long enough to show Maggie that his time was more valuable than hers—though she knew his salary, and it most definitely was not.

"Boss man needs me," she continued as soon as the typing had stopped. "I'm not sure how long I'll be gone, so any fires that come up in the vicinity of Levi Ferris…*you* put them out, okay?"

Neil took a moment to consider what Maggie had said, as if weighing his options and deciding whether to help her out or not. "All right. I'll hold down the fort."

When Maggie pulled up to the fuel stop, Levi was already waiting outside clutching a bulging shopping bag to his chest. He was covered in oily black smears and dusty patches of desert sand. Maggie guessed he must have had some car trouble and tried to work on it himself—without success, it seemed. He hurriedly finished off a large carton of orange juice, which he proceeded to drop onto the concrete. There was a crazed look in his eyes and an unreal smile plastered across his face.

If this guy weren't her boss, Maggie would have turned the car around right then. Instead, she parked and reluctantly unlocked the door for him.

"Thank God you got here before the cops!" he said, climbing in. "I was beginning to wonder, you know?"

That's a hell of a greeting. Maggie needed a moment to catch up.

"Well, *drive*, damn it!" Levi continued. "Seriously, we need to move. I'm sure they've identified my car by now, so no going back to the office just yet. I'll need you to take these and keep them safe for me." He placed his shopping bag on the floor in front of him and gestured toward its contents.

Maggie couldn't look very closely while also attempting to exit the parking lot, but the bag appeared to be filled with smaller plastic bags of…*Oh, God.* "Is that the dreck?"

"It's…*most* of it."

"What happened to the rest? Where's the briefcase?"

Levi rolled his window down a bit, pulled the lenses out of his eyes, and casually tossed them out onto the street. "That'll buy us a *little* time. We need to talk."

No shit we need to talk! "I agree. More specifically, *you* need to talk, Levi. What's this about cops? What did you do?"

"None of that is actually important. That's what I need to tell you. None of *this* is important." He waved his arms around wildly, causing Maggie to swerve a little. "And call me Lucky, please."

Maggie glanced over to check if he was serious about that. He appeared to be.

Levi continued after a moment: "Find someplace to park. This is big, important stuff here. Or else it's nothing. I can't really be sure."

Great. He's finally cracked. "It's important…that nothing is important?" Maggie couldn't resist playing along.

"Pretty much," Levi replied straight-faced. "Just find us a spot to…Look, there! Park close to the road." He pointed to a big-box megamall with a mostly full parking lot.

Once they had come to a complete stop, Levi took a breath and continued: "Okay. I think I remember some things, but they don't—*at first blush*—seem to make a whole lot of sense.

It may sound like I'm talking pseudophilosophical hooey here, so bear with me."

"I'm bearing with you pretty hard," Maggie said. Levi didn't seem to notice the edge in her tone.

"Good." He smiled, revealing some of that black gunk still stuck in his teeth. "Now imagine for a moment that time travel is actually possible. What does that say about the nature of the universe?"

"I've heard this sort of thing before. You're not gonna start talking about multiple universes, are you?"

"No, that's a load of crap, obviously. I'm talking about what we're living in right now. The universe!" He gesticulated some more, obviously frustrated at the inadequacy of words. "If there's more to it than we know, then all that should just be added to our definition of *the* universe."

"Predestination then?"

"Predestination falls apart as soon as you become aware of it and start changing things. No, just bear *with* me here!"

He paused a moment to make sure there wouldn't be any more little interruptions. Maggie kept quiet. *Whatever he needs to get his crazies out.*

"What I'm saying is…remembering feels like time travel, right? Dreaming works the same way. Well, what if that's all we have in the first place? Thoughts arranged in time. And we're free—if we can only learn *how*—to change those thoughts around all we like. So no predestination. One world. One ever-changing universe. And *we* can change it! Past, present, future… The key to it all is *dreck*! It's not actually *from* this world at all. I mean, this level…this dream! It—it—it *starts* the dream. Sets it up. And now we're dreaming about *it*. Do you follow me?"

"You're right," Maggie said. Levi looked hopeful. "It sounds like hooey."

"Do you have a better explanation for…Oh, all right. I hear you. What I need you to do is *try* the dreck. Like a spoonful should do it."

"Oh, hell no. Not me. I can't—"

"Of course you can! Look at me!" Levi raised his eyebrows, grinned maniacally, and did something like jazz hands on either side of his face.

"Exactly!" Maggie countered. "You need *help*, Levi. You're falling apart, and I have to assume that's from the dreck. Am I right?"

"More from the wreck," he said. "Which had nothing to do with the dreck! Honest."

Maggie still had her doubts.

Levi glanced furtively around the lot and said, "Listen, I have to get going now. I *need* you to do this for me." He looked her squarely in the eyes. "You're my go-to right hand, right? I can trust you?"

"Sure, absolutely, but—"

"*I* need to know I'm not crazy as much as you do. More so, actually."

This did nothing to convince Maggie, but she nodded demurely, mostly to be rid of him.

"That's my gal!" And with that, Levi got out of the car and started his trek across the lot to the megamall.

There on the floor of the passenger side sat a leaky plastic bag full of the theomimetic substance known as dreck. Maggie stared at the black puddle that was forming there, trying to decide what to do.

"Shit."

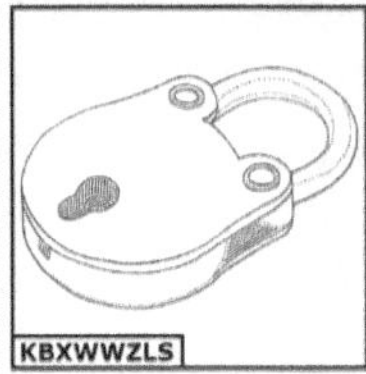

5. STORY

"ARE YOU REALLY SURE YOU WANT TO DO THIS?" MAGGIE asked in that condescending tone of hers.

Neil Conrad had made up his mind. Back at his girlfriend Violet's house in Memorial Park, under the watchful care of both Violet and that corporate climber Maggie Moon, he was finally going to try the mysterious substance known as dreck. With a bravado he hoped didn't sound too forced, he said, "Bring it on," and gave a thumbs-up.

"Half a teaspoon *only*," said Violet.

"Right," added Maggie. "No need to go totally off the rails on your first trip."

Neil carefully measured out a half-teaspoon of the syrupy stuff, loudly proclaimed, "For science!" and then gulped it down.

In actuality, this was Neil's first time to try an illicit drug of any sort. He'd always seen himself as a real straight-arrow type, no funny business. But here was a chance to help the boss out in his hour of need, and of course Levi would be grateful. He'd also be well aware that it was Neil, not Maggie, who'd taken the bullet for him. Neil would make absolutely certain of that.

"Feeling anything yet?" asked Maggie, laptop open, ready to take notes.

"I'll let you know when I…Hm. Maybe there is something," he said. "It could be nothing, but…my mind is starting to wander."

Maggie started clacking away on her keyboard.

Violet leaned in closer to Neil and said, "Close your eyes and tell us what you see."

Neil squinted, and his eyes began to dart back and forth like he was deep in dream sleep. "It's raining," he began. "I'm a kid again, back in my old room getting ready for school. It's early in the morning. The rain clears up before it's time to leave. The water in our ditch outside is just shy of overflowing. The level starts to drop as all the water rushes downhill.

"I wait for the bus a good half hour before concluding that school is out for the day. I tell my mom and hop on my bike to go celebrate with my friend Tommy down the street.

"My neighborhood is really just a one-mile loop of narrow road, lined with mobile homes and dropped into a thick pine forest. Heading down the hill to Tommy's house, the road keeps curving to the right, so I can't see very far ahead. My tires hit water as I go around a bend, and I'm too excited by the novelty of all this to see the danger I'm in. Before I know it, I'm holding onto my bike with one hand and treading water with the other to keep afloat in the rushing flood.

"After a few long seconds, I let go of my bike so I can grab onto the luggage rack of a van that's almost entirely underwater. The current is pulling at me hard, trying to send me into the woods. I can see a massive whirlpool churning there at the edge of the forest, maybe a hundred feet away. That thing would pull me down under the water pretty quick, I realize.

"I pull myself up onto the roof of the van and sit there, soaked and stunned. Across what used to be the street, Tommy and his family are stranded on the roof of what used to be their house. All we can do is wave at each other.

"I just sit there unable to decide what to do until Tommy stands up and calls out to me. 'Hey, Neil!' he says. I think it's kind of funny, him yelling like that, but I call back, 'Hey, Tommy!' 'Use the trees!' he says. 'Behind you!' And he's pantomiming like I can hop from one tree to the next like a squirrel or something. It takes me a minute to get it.

"He's trying to tell me to swim from tree to tree, and I can see what he means. The water's gonna get more shallow if I head that way a little, away from Tommy's house. I leave my shoes on top of the van and swim against the current from one tree to the next until the water is finally shallow enough to wade through."

For a moment, Neil rested in the satisfaction that he'd brought the story to its conclusion. But no, something wasn't sitting right. There were other memories of that flood—*different* memories of the *same* time. "Wait. That's not how it happened."

Violet stroked his arm, encouraging him to go on. Maggie continued taking notes.

"Tommy wasn't there that day. I waited on the top of that van for a while, but it started raining again, and I was worried the water would keep rising until I had nowhere to sit. I started swimming back the way I'd come, but I—I couldn't fight the current. I kept moving backward no matter how hard I paddled until I finally just let myself get swept toward the trees, thinking I'd grab onto one of them and be okay. But the whirlpool…It pulled me under. I couldn't stay afloat for anything; I just—I finally breathed in the water, and…I died."

Maggie looked up from her laptop as if to make sure he wasn't putting her on. "You *died*?"

Neil opened his eyes. "How can I remember that?" he asked no one in particular.

"That didn't really happen," said Violet. "Obviously."

"No, it really did," Neil insisted. "I died that time, but then I went back, and…I guess I was able to fix it? This stuff is weird. Nothing seems *real* right now. Like it's all just a bunch of stories."

Violet gave him a hug. "Just keep calm. I'm here for you. I'm real. You're real."

Neil looked at Violet with fresh eyes. He knew her, but she wasn't his girlfriend. He knew her from work. *Dr. Violet Valdez.* "You're a…a doctor! Some kind of psychologist. What are you trying to do to me?"

"Neil, listen to me," Violet said firmly. "I'm not a doctor. I'm still in college. The dreck is giving you weird ideas."

Dr. Frederick Foster. "Who's Frederick Foster?" The name caught Maggie's attention, which seemed to confirm Neil's suspicion. "What *is* this? You know a Dr. Foster, Maggie?"

Maggie closed her laptop and said, "Calm down, Neil. I don't know any Dr. Foster. I used to know a guy with that name is all. Not a doctor."

Neil was unconvinced. "I feel like…like I can hear your thoughts now. This stuff made me psychic. Go on, take some more notes! That's important."

Violet looked worried. "Neil, I don't think—"

"Think of a number between one and ten, both of you." He looked into their eyes in turn, first Violet and then Maggie. This time, the messages were more visual, but he could picture their numbers clear as day. He pointed at Violet and said, "Eight." Then at Maggie. "Two."

Maggie said, "Nope," and Violet just shook her head.

Liars. Neil tried to keep his anger from showing on his face. If they wanted to pretend like he was just imagining things, then he could continue the research on his own. "Okay, maybe it's just the dreck talking. Don't mind me. I feel like…maybe I should sleep it off?" He turned to Maggie. "Would that be okay? I'll report any weird dreams back to you, if I can remember them."

Maggie looked a little disappointed, but Violet spoke up: "Absolutely, babe. If you feel like you need to sleep it off, then that's what you should do."

Yeah, right. There was no way Neil could sleep on this stuff. He felt like every cell in his body was alive with independent consciousness. He doubted there had ever been a dreck user as capable as himself to decode its manifold secrets. He just needed some time alone to listen and meditate without interference. There were so many possibilities to explore now. *And precious little time to do it.*

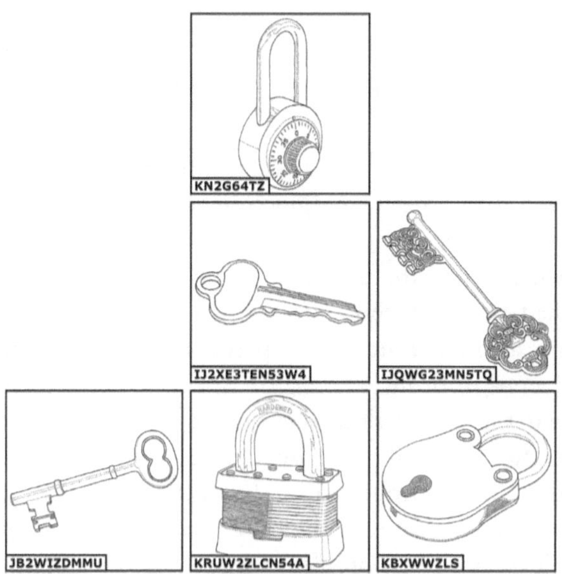

6. BURNDOWN

VIOLET COULDN'T STAY IN THE HOUSE A MINUTE LONGER.
She was feeling restless and worried about Neil, afraid that damn
dreck might mess him up permanently. After all the time she'd
spent trying to convince him to loosen up and smoke a little weed
with her, he'd certainly agreed to sample this mystery drug pretty
quickly. *Maybe he has a thing for Maggie,* she thought, surprising
herself how little she actually minded the idea. *Honestly though,
Neil would eat her alive.*

Violet opened the bedroom door a crack, letting a beam of
light fall across Neil's face. As far as she could tell, he was asleep.
She'd never known him to meditate. *He doesn't need me to watch
over him like a baby.*

"Hey, Maggie?"

Maggie looked up from her computer but didn't actually say
anything.

"I'm gonna take a little walk, okay? You okay here? Like if Neil wakes up, you'll make sure he doesn't do anything stupid?"

"Sure, no problem," she said, returning to her typing.

"Green. If you need anything, just ping me."

It was the perfect time for an evening walk. Fully past sundown to avoid the dog-walkers, not so late that the corner stores had closed up shop already. Not that Violet intended to patronize a corner store on this particular evening. Tonight she needed a proper drink.

Down the steady slope she walked—past the houses, the bakery, the junkyard, that one place with all those surreal sculptures in the front yard... *This walk's gonna be so much tougher coming back,* she thought. *Especially if I wind up getting drunk.* It wouldn't be a problem though. She'd staggered up that hill more times than she could count. The struggle was actually comforting in a way. Something to fight against, even if it was only gravity. Violet was in control of the situation. Whatever resistance the universe put in her way, she was ready to kick its ass. *Just let a mugger try and touch me.* She gripped the stun gun in her pocket with satisfaction.

Violet looked up at the perfectly full moon. Just a big dead rock floating there doing nothing. But it never ceased to be beautiful somehow. *Maybe that's what makes it beautiful,* she considered. *It's not trying to be something it's not.* Earth, on the other hand, was straining pretty hard, always scrambling to remake itself in the image of some sci-fi dystopia from the golden age of ersatz coffee and mutton chop sideburns. *When will it be enough?*

Overlooking the irony inherent in using technology to complain about technology, she used her lenses to open up Dunk, a social news app that was a guilty pleasure of hers. She scrolled through the trending outrages as she walked, looking for just the right story to satisfy her wistful, technophobic mood. By the time she arrived at Epoptica, her favorite neighborhood bar slash coffee shop, she was well into the weeds of an online debate centered around Neil and Maggie's boss, Levi Ferris. Ferris had been arrested for his involvement in a hit-and-run accident with some poor guy on a motorcycle named Frederick Foster. *Why does that name sound familiar?* Violet had already pieced together much of the story from what Maggie had told her, but she hadn't known Ferris had actually *killed* a guy!

Using up all her reserve creds in the app, she dunked hard on Levi Ferris. This one wasn't just for poor dead Freddy Foster; it was for Neil too, back home languishing on the same dreck that probably caused the accident in the first place. No doubt Ferris had been sampling the goods. Why else would he just wander off like that, leaving his car behind?

As usual, there were a fair number of trolls and sycophants giving the offender a "pass" for one reason or another, but still, the score stayed firmly in "dunk" territory. Those people just liked to be contrarians, Violet suspected. Still, the arguments they put forward on Ferris's behalf would likely be dressed up and regurgitated before a judge to get Ferris a lenient sentence. He probably wouldn't do any jail time at all, not with the perennial War on Drugs in full force. Too many dope smokers and pill poppers to lock up instead.

"There ain't no justice," Violet said aloud, taking a seat at the empty bar.

"How do you mean?" asked the bartender, a stocky, unassuming type named Wayne.

"I mean some tech billionaire runs down a kid on a bike, and what happens? The kid's family probably has to pay to fix the bastard's car."

Wayne laughed and looked a little scandalized. "You sound like you need a *real* drink tonight. No coffee."

"Damn straight, no coffee," Violet agreed. "I came here for the mead! Give me that dark one."

"Ah yes, excellent choice." Wayne opened up a bottle of bochet and poured some in a wine glass for Violet.

"The thing that gets me," Violet said between sips, "is just how *normal* all this stuff is." She waved her fingers around her eyes as if all the universe were contained within her lenses—or at least the parts of the universe that bothered her. "I can't disconnect, you know? It's like a *drug*. For one reason or another, I keep coming back."

Wayne gestured toward his own eyes in guilty solidarity. "I know just what you mean. I don't have to drink every day. I don't need coffee every day. But I can't go an hour without checking my feed."

"You know, I probably shouldn't say anything, but…some of these tech companies…They're branching out, you know?" Violet was buzzing already as Wayne poured her second glass. "Have you heard of *dreck*?" she asked in a conspiratorial whisper.

"As a matter of fact," Wayne said, "My roommate won't shut up about it lately. It's supposed to, you know…reveal the secrets of the universe and all that."

"It's bioengineering married with nanotech." Violet took another couple of gulps to finish off glass number two. "And who knows what that means for brain chemistry? I don't trust it. Or anyone on it. That stuff'll mess you up."

Wayne listened politely as Violet ranted on about Triclave United and all the evils of the modern world. He seemed fully sympathetic to her cause, but in the end, maybe he was just doing his job. The booze kept flowing, after all.

Eventually, without much caring about the consequences, Violet started posting bits of what she knew on Dunk. Her fans were eating it up, bumping her posts higher and higher in the stack. Before she knew it, she'd spilled every piece of inside information she had on Ferris, Triclave, and dreck—and quite a bit more, actually, filling in gaps with more-or-less educated guesses.

"Hey, Wayne?" she said after finishing off the last of the bochet.

"What can I get for you?"

"I'm thinking…I could actually use some coffee now."

7. SPRINT

JUST ABOUT CLOSING TIME, THOUGHT WAYNE PARK AS HE gave the empty tables a final wipe-down. He also needed to clean the bar before calling it a night, but Violet had her head laid down on it, using her arm as a pillow, and she didn't look like she was going anywhere. Not without some sober assistance.

Violet had been a regular at Epoptica for longer than Wayne had been working there, and she'd never camped out like this before. Something was obviously bothering her. Something about dreck for sure, but also…social media? Tech in general? She was always a little hard to follow once she got going on a rant. He found this pretty adorable, in a scary sort of way.

Wayne had a bit of a crush on Violet, though he knew she had a boyfriend. Where was that guy when she needed him though? They couldn't be all that close, it seemed. And anyway, it wasn't like they were *married*.

"I'm about to close up here in a minute…You need a ride home?" Wayne asked as casually as he could manage.

Violet raised her head, giving Wayne a probing look. "You're a real *gentleman* type, ain't you?"

Wayne laughed nervously. "I, um…I *try* to—"

"No, that's good, I mean," Violet mumbled. "Or at least… it's not *bad*."

She still hadn't answered the question. Wayne waited a moment and tried again: "So, can I give you a ride?"

"Yeah, that'd be nice, actually. I'm not far, but it's all uphill." She drank the last bit of her coffee. The cold dregs. "Thanks. I'm pretty tired."

The parking lot behind Epoptica was empty, aside from Wayne's car and a few stray beer cans. A couple of cats were sniffing around the dumpster, but they ran away when Wayne and Violet walked past.

"What are you doing, Vi?" called a figure from the shadows.

Violet jumped and shouted, "Neil! What the hell, man?! Trying to give me a heart attack?"

Wayne reached into his pocket, fumbling for his keys as the man approached. He remembered hearing somewhere that you could stop an attacker by letting your keys poke out between the fingers of your fist and going for the eyes. He shuddered at the idea but gripped the keys anyway.

Neil continued, "What are you doing with this asshole? You were gonna get in his car?"

Violet hesitated, so Wayne spoke up: "Look, I wasn't going to…I mean, really, she just needed a ride up the hill, so…"

"So you thought you'd play the hero," Neil said. "I get it, man. Really. I understand so much more than you'd ever believe. I'll tell you a secret…" He stepped a little closer. "I can actually *hear* what you're thinking." He glared at Wayne, ignoring Violet as she yelled for him to calm down. Neil took another step closer, keeping his eyes fixed on Wayne's. He clearly didn't like what he saw.

Wayne put out a hand and backed up, struggling to come up with a polite way to tell Neil that he was mistaken about reading his mind. "Seriously, man, I wasn't—"

Before he could finish the thought, he saw a flash of white and realized he'd just taken a punch to the face. Blood trickled into his mouth and down his chin. It had happened so fast that Wayne actually felt more confusion than pain. No time for pain yet. *This guy's gonna kill me,* he thought. *Right here in the parking lot.*

"Could be," answered Neil, drawing back for another blow. But before he could land a second punch, his face froze in a momentary rictus, and then he fell to the ground howling with pain. Violet stood behind him, a stun gun in her hand. "Start the car!" she yelled, hovering over Neil with the weapon in case he tried to get back up.

Wayne didn't need to be told twice. He ran straight to his car, hastily started it up, and sped away just as Violet was climbing into the passenger side. "Buckle up! Buckle up!" he shouted before her door was even shut. "Are you okay?"

"Am *I* okay?" Violet echoed. "You're the one bleeding every-where! Are you good to drive?"

"Yeah yeah yeah, I'm good. This is just… Wait, where should I go?"

"Forget taking me home, I guess," said Violet. "Take a left on the freeway. I'll figure something out."

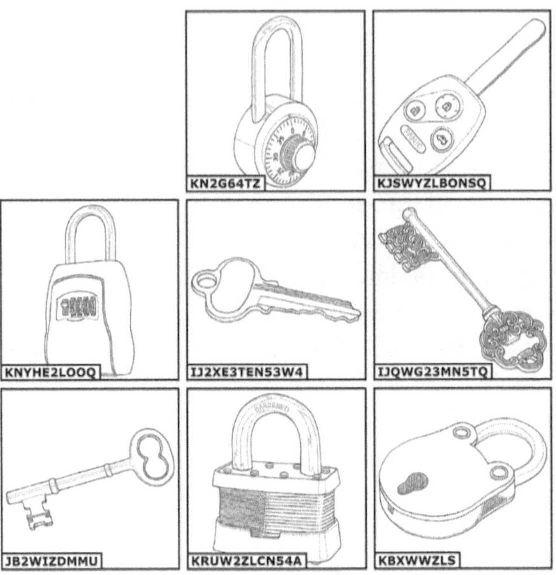

8. Release

LAILA DUCHAMP WANDERED THROUGH THE SPARSE BIRCH forest, holding onto tree after tree for support. The muddy ground felt like molasses, clinging to her feet with each step. In the hazy amber evening sky, she could just barely make out the glow of a full moon through the trees ahead. She followed it dutifully, her only compass in an endless sea of homogeneity.

"The only way out is through," Laila told herself.

"Not so," called a familiar voice a few steps behind her. "We can get out of this anytime you decide to wake up." It was Flip Foster, her self-proclaimed psychopomp spirit guide.

"Flip," said Laila wearily. "Always a pleasure. But actually… it's not a dream this time."

"It's *always* a dream," he insisted with a devilish grin. "As many times as we've 'woken up' into just another layer of dreaming, I'd expect you'd remember that by now."

Laila clicked her tongue and resumed staring at the moon. "Okay, fine. But look, Flip…Whether it's real or not, I've still got to *treat* it like it's real."

Flip looked a little wounded. "I never said it wasn't *real*. I mean, real is subjective. Take me, for example. I can't prove it to you, but *I* know I'm real. Even if I can't be sure exactly who or what I am, I still have to exist somewhere. Right? I think; therefore, I am."

"Sure," answered Laila in a placating tone. "That's what I'm saying, actually. You tell me I'm dreaming, but all I know is I exist *here*. I can't remember anything beyond that. So it's real enough."

"It's easy to forget," Flip muttered, absently picking at some peeling paper-white bark. "Context-dependent memory. Whenever I go back, I always forget how it ends…"

"What do you mean? How what ends?"

"God, I thought I'd have more time. All the time in the world." Flip stared up at the moon as if struggling to recognize his own face in the mirror. "I died this morning."

Laila kept quiet. She wanted to object, but Flip was actually making sense in a creepy sort of way. She didn't doubt him, even if it meant she had to doubt everything else.

"I can't keep holding on and pretending like that didn't happen," he continued. "This is as far as I can go. I'm done."

And with that, Laila found herself alone again in the endless forest. She tried to keep moving but found herself waist deep in the sticky black mud. It was nearly impossible to wade through it. She looked up at the clear night sky and found the full moon, which was now directly overhead. *Well, that's no help,* she thought. *If only I could locate the North Star…*Through the bare limbs of birch trees, she scanned the starry sky and was startled to find one of the stars looking back at her.

"H-h-hello?" Laila asked, her voice shaking.

Don't be afraid, replied the star. Its voice bypassed Laila's ears and touched her mind directly. *Don't be afraid to open your eyes.*

Laila understood this advice perfectly well. It was as if she were talking to herself. She took a deep breath and forced her eyes to open, replacing the starry night sky with the beige ceiling of her bedroom.

Just then, there was a knock on the door of her apartment. "What the hell?" she muttered. *Don't be afraid,* echoed her dream.

She'd fallen asleep with her lenses in again. It was 1:12 in the morning. And there was a ping from Violet: "I'm really sorry to bother you so late. Is it okay if I come over? It's a long story, but I can't go home right now."

"Sure," Laila replied as another knock sounded on her door. *Don't be afraid.* She dragged herself out of bed and shuffled over to the door. Through the peephole, she could see Violet, but standing beside her was a chubby guy whose shirt appeared to be covered in blood. "What the hell, Vi?" Laila messaged back without touching the door. "Are you okay? Who's that guy?"

"He's harmless! He just had a nosebleed."

Laila sighed heavily, turned the deadbolt, and opened the door. "Hey, Vi," she said without enthusiasm. "Who's your friend?"

The guy smiled, revealing blood on his teeth. "I'm Wayne," he said quietly. "Sorry about this."

"Okay, here's what's going on," Violet started, obviously drunk. "Neil just came up and punched him in the nose 'cause I was going to get a ride home 'cause I was drinking a lot 'cause Neil tried this new drug, and I was worried about him, actually. Yeah! But then he punched Wayne, and I was like, 'Nope,' and I got him with my stun gun."

"Yeah, that's about it," added a much more sober Wayne. "Can I use your bathroom?"

Laila pointed to the open bathroom door. Something about Wayne reminded her of the dream she'd been having when they came and woke her up. No, that wasn't right…She'd woken *herself* up. Somebody had told her to open her eyes. *Don't be afraid.*

"Do you know dreck?" asked Violet.

"You mean like…the drug? I've heard of it," Laila said without much interest.

"That's what Neil is on. And earlier today, this big executive from Triclave—that's Neil's company—this guy was high on dreck, and he ran down some poor kid on a bike. Phil…No, *Fred*. Freddy…Frederick Foster."

Wayne turned off the water and awkwardly dried his face with a wad of toilet paper. "Wait, what did you say? Frederick Foster? That's my roommate's name! He goes by Flip though. What happened?"

"Flip died this morning," Laila replied automatically. Then hearing her own words, she remembered more of her dream. *Don't be afraid to open your eyes.*

And so she took a breath and did just that.

Suddenly, Laila was lost at sea. Wherever she looked was water and more water, black and thick like molasses. Above her head was a moonless night sky. The featureless expanse both above and below was enough to give her vertigo. She had no idea which way to swim, and it was all she could manage just to stay afloat in the dark, viscous liquid.

Gradually, she came to notice a gentle current pulling her round and round in circles and drawing her feet toward the center. She tried her best to swim out of the whirlpool, but it was no use. The current's direction kept shifting around her in the pitch darkness, faster and faster on each pass. *I'm going to sink,* she thought in a panic. *I'm going to drown, unless…unless this is a dream.*

It's always *a dream.*

Terrified but hopeful, Laila gave in and let herself sink below the surface at last. She held her breath for as long as she could manage and then, when she could stand it no longer, breathed in the darkness just like it was air. It burned at first, and her heart pounded violently, but then…

She was okay. She wasn't even underwater any longer. She

could feel herself in bed, waking up. *Ugh, one of those multilevel dreams. I hate those.*

Laila opened her eyes to an unfamiliar room with no windows and very minimal furnishings. It was freezing, so she tugged at her thin blanket. The bottom of it was sewn directly to the mattress cover. If you could call that rigid three-inch-thick pad a mattress. And the pillow wasn't any better. It was the size of a book and felt like it was stuffed with blue jeans. This was definitely some sort of a mental health facility. She was familiar with places like this, though she couldn't remember why.

She sat up to discover she was wearing nothing but disposable blue scrubs and a plastic band on her wrist bearing the number 946. There was a white bathrobe on the floor beside her bed, so she threw it on over her scrubs to warm up.

She wandered through an open door out into the hall. Identical doors ran up and down the featureless passage. They were all open, but no lights were on inside the rooms. All the patients appeared to be sleeping. Laila passed a dozen or so such rooms before coming to one labeled "CHAPEL." She looked inside and was startled to lock eyes with an older man in scrubs like her own.

"Laila!" he said. "You're up early. Remember me? Tommy. Tommy Blick?"

"Sorry, no," she answered. "I don't remember anything." The man did look familiar, but only because he reminded her of Flip Foster in some subtle way she couldn't pin down.

"Well, now, maybe that's for the best. They say if we forget the past, then we're doomed to repeat it, but the word 'doomed' is a bit strong, I'd say. It's just the eternal return. You've got to fall in love with Fate. Imagine Sisyphus happy. Am I right?"

Laila smiled despite her misgivings about the situation. "I'm sure you are. But right now, I need to get my bearings so I can find a way out of here. I'm not supposed to be here."

"And I am?" Tommy shot back.

"I didn't mean—"

"Really, it depends on who's doing the supposing. Plenty of people suppose us dead. This place is a tomb."

"I'm sorry, I wasn't trying to—"

"I do know a way out though, if that's what you want. I mean, if you're *sure*. You stay in here, you've got it made in the shade. Three hots and a cot. Out there, well, you're on your own."

"I've been on my own before," Laila said, though she wasn't sure when that would have been. "Show me."

Tommy grinned. This was obviously the answer he'd been hoping for. He gestured for Laila to follow and led her to the far end of the room, to what looked like a disused fireplace. He moved aside a black iron grating and said, "You can climb right up to the roof, and from there…you'll see."

Laila crawled into the open shaft of this ancient chimney, and sure enough, there was a wooden ladder propped up against its back wall. She considered thanking Tommy, but that didn't feel appropriate somehow. "So long," she said.

"Good luck," he answered, replacing the iron grating.

In the pitch darkness of the chimney shaft, Laila climbed the ladder, rung after rung, until she bumped her head on a thin metal covering, which revealed a flash of daylight as it was momentarily lifted. Keeping hold of the ladder with one hand, she carefully moved the chimney cover with the other and then pulled herself up onto the roof of the building.

Standing, Laila blinked in the sunlight to let her eyes adjust. She now found herself at the top of a Mesoamerican pyramid, something like the Pyramid of the Moon in Teotihuacan. Except at the bottom of this structure, she saw no ancient ruins, no verdant fields or jungle. There were ordinary city blocks with office buildings, megamalls, and elevated freeways winding their way throughout it all. Thousands of vehicles flowed steadily this way and that like streams of multicolored ants.

A long-forgotten Bible passage crept into her consciousness: *All these things I will give to you…*

"Dreck," Laila said aloud. "You can keep it."

She took a deep breath and forced her eyes to open once more, replacing her view of the city with the familiar surroundings of HiVE lab 2374. This had never happened before. She'd actually woken up on her own.

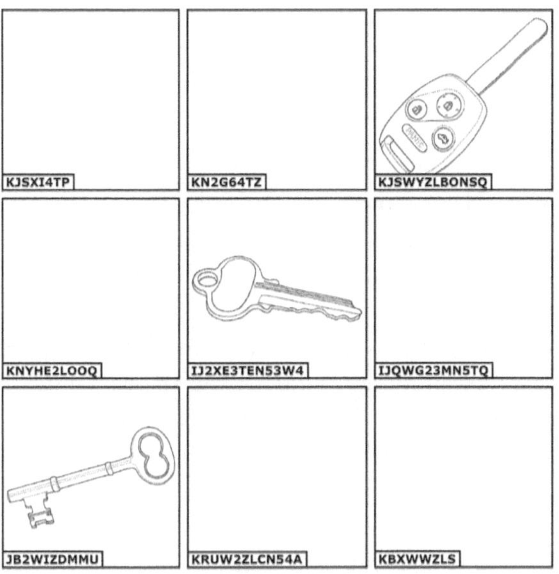

9. RETRO

LEVI KEPT HIS EYES SHUT DESPITE THE INCESSANT BEEPING coming from his headset. His bed shifted back into the shape of a chair, his overhead lamp turned on, and the HiVE lab returned to life. Once the sim was over, the system was intent on waking everyone up, no matter what time it was.

The last thing Levi remembered from the other side was lying on his cot in the El Paso County lock-up trying to fall asleep. Coming down off the dreck hadn't been easy, particularly in that inhospitable setting. And now his own equipment was conspiring against him to ensure he had about the worst night's sleep of his life. His mouth still burned with the lingering aftertaste of Homeostatic Neurointegrative Elixir, a sickly-sweet concoction more often referred to as HNE, or "honey." It couldn't have been all that long since he'd taken his dose and connected to the HiVE.

"Hey, Tommy…" Levi said to bring up his digital assistant. "What time is it?"

"The time is now 4:05."

He popped his smartlenses back in and checked his feed. "What ended the sim so early?" he asked, almost to himself.

"Your student Laila Duchamp aborted neurointegration following a series of—"

"Bye, Tommy." Levi was already reading the report. There was no need to announce the details to the whole class. "I'll be damned," he muttered. Laila had woken herself up. Maybe she actually *was* ready to graduate.

"Levi, you asshole!" Flip Foster shouted, jumping up from his seat across the room. "You did it *again!*"

Levi put up his hands and shrank back a little. "Yeah, I'm sorry about that," was all he could think to say.

"Do you just subconsciously want to murder me or what?!"

Levi couldn't help but crack a smile. "I'm not sure it works that way."

Violet started laughing. "I'm pretty sure that's *exactly* how it works."

"It could just as easily be *you* that wants me to kill him," Levi countered. "The course of the sim is determined by everyone collectively."

"What's going on now?" asked Neil. "I can't remember a thing."

"Never mind the drama," said Levi. "We're all up early because Laila actually forced herself awake, which ended the sim. Well done, Laila."

Violet gave a sarcastic slow clap, which was soon joined in earnest by Wayne and then Flip. Everyone stared at Laila, who was motionless in her seat, a hand over her eyes to shield them from the light of her station's overhead lamp.

Maggie walked over to Levi, a look of concern on her face. "So that's it then, right? She's got to graduate now?"

"Not necessarily," Levi said. "Though when I first woke myself up, yeah, I was slated to graduate within a couple of days." He turned toward Laila. "But this doesn't have to be the end. There's always grad school. And then if that goes well…"

Finally, Laila spoke up: "I'd actually *like* to graduate and just be done with the HiVE. I'm tired of making the same mistakes over and over just because of some subconscious fears or desires or whatever. I want to get back to my *real* life. I want to dream my own dreams again."

The room fell silent. Graduation wasn't something to look forward to. It meant an end to the freedom of living a fresh life each night immune to the terrors of the waking world. If you died outside of a HiVE simulation, you died for real. As far as anybody knew, that was it. Maybe there was more waiting for you beyond the veil—eternal paradise even—but maybe not. Better the devil you know than the one you don't.

"Now, Laila…" Levi began. "Are you sure about this? You've done really well here, and I can put in a recommendation for you to—"

"I'm sure."

Flip walked over to Laila's station and quietly asked, "Can we talk about this?"

She smiled, but it didn't reach her eyes. "Go ahead. It's not like we have any secrets here. Everything we've ever experienced in the HiVE, life after life after life…It's all just *data*, right? It's all going into Levi's thesis."

"Okay, here goes." Flip took a deep breath. "I care about you. I want to stick with you wherever you go. If that means getting old and dying just the *one* more time, then that's what I want. I can handle it."

Laila took his hand and smiled for real. "Slow down, dude. We still have as much time as we've ever had. I just want to try living at full speed for a while."

CLIFF JONES JR.

is a rising star in the world of dreampunk/irrealist literature, though he has quite a ways yet to rise. In both his writing career and his day job as a software developer, he leans heavily on his background in linguistics and years of teaching experience. Neurodivergence has been a major theme of Cliff's life: growing up with a profoundly autistic brother, helping to raise a daughter on the spectrum, and of course, navigating his own atypical neurochemistry. This may be why he places such a high value on internal worlds and alternative modes of experience. Find him online at *CliffJonesJr.com*. Say hello! He's actually quite friendly.

www.ingramcontent.com/pod-product-compliance
Lightning Source LLC
Chambersburg PA
CBHW020045310726
48970CB00007B/2418